NO-
THANKS
Thanksgiving

By Ilene Cooper

THE HOLIDAY FIVE

NO-THANKS
Thanksgiving

BY ILENE COOPER

VIKING

VIKING
Published by the Penguin Group
Penguin Books USA Inc., 375 Hudson Street, New York, New York 10014, U.S.A.
Penguin Books Ltd, 27 Wrights Lane, London W8 5TZ, England
Penguin Books Australia Ltd, Ringwood, Victoria, Australia
Penguin Books Canada Ltd, 10 Alcorn Avenue, Toronto, Ontario, Canada M4V 3B2
Penguin Books (N.Z.) Ltd, 182–190 Wairau Road, Auckland 10, New Zealand

Penguin Books Ltd, Registered Offices: Harmondsworth, Middlesex, England

First published in 1996 by Viking, a division of Penguin Books USA Inc.

1   3   5   7   9   10   8   6   4   2

LIBRARY OF CONGRESS CATALOGING-IN-PUBLICATION DATA
Cooper, Ilene.
No-thanks Thanksgiving / by Ilene Cooper.
p.   cm.—(The Holiday Five)
Summary: Five friends from summer camp renew their relationship over the
holidays with a trip to New York City.
ISBN 0-670-85657-6 (hardcover)
[1. Friendship—Fiction.   2.Thanksgiving—Fiction.   3. New York (N.Y.)—Fiction.]
I. Title.   II. Series: Cooper, Ilene. Holiday Five.

PZ7.C7856No   1996   [Fic]—dc20   96-17080   CIP   AC

Printed in U.S.A.
Set in Century

NO-
THANKS
Thanksgiving

ONE

"Better get up. The waffles are getting cold."

Kathy Wallace glanced over at her stepsister Anne, who was making her bed. Kathy was still under the covers, and just watching the efficient pillow plumping made her want to roll over. She and Anne were as close as any two people who share a bedroom every other weekend, and little else. Not very.

"What time are you going home?" Anne asked bluntly. "Some of my friends are coming over to study this afternoon, and we'll need the room."

"I'll be on the one o'clock train," Kathy said, getting out of bed. "Early enough for you?"

Anne didn't seem to notice the sarcasm. "That's fine."

Kathy usually stayed later at her father's high-rise apartment on Sundays, but today Dr. Wallace was going out of town, so there was no reason for her to hang around. It would only mean more time with her stepmother, Marion, her little half sister, Helena, and of course, Anne. She'd just as soon get back to Lake Pointe, the Chicago suburb where she lived with her mother.

Anne put on a pair of silver shell earrings. "Have you seen these?" she asked. "I got them in New York."

"Nice," Kathy responded curtly. Anne's trip to New York was something of a sore point. Marion's sister, Zoe, used to live in Chicago, but she'd moved to New York City over the summer. Despite the fact that she was actually Anne's aunt, not Kathy's, Zoe and Kathy had a great relationship. Truth be told, Kathy liked Zoe better than Marion and Anne put together. Zoe had invited both Anne and Kathy to New York, but Anne had managed to finagle the trip for a weekend that Kathy couldn't go, and in place of Kathy, Anne had taken her best friend. Oh, Zoe had promised that she could come another time and bring a friend as well, but Kathy had her doubts as to whether that would actually ever happen.

As Kathy was getting out of bed, four-year-old

Helena bounded into the room. "We are all waiting for you," she scolded. Although Helena was getting more tolerable as she got older, bossiness was still one of her main characteristics.

"I'm going to take a shower and get dressed. Tell Marion and Dad they don't have to wait for me. I'm not hungry anyway."

They must have taken her seriously, because by the time Kathy arrived at the breakfast table, only one lonely waffle remained on the platter. Now that most of the food was gone, Kathy felt hungry after all.

"Do you want some milk with that?" Marion asked, as Kathy stabbed the remaining waffle and put it on her plate.

Kathy nodded, and Marion handed the pitcher of milk over to her.

"I'll drop you off at the train station on my way to the airport," Dr. Wallace said.

"Where are you going?" Kathy asked. Lately, he'd been traveling a lot, and it was getting difficult to keep up with his schedule.

"To a medical convention in Oregon. I'm giving a speech on hip replacements."

"Mmm," was the only comment Kathy could think to make.

The phone rang, and Helena jumped up to answer it. Answering the phone was one of her favorite things. "Wallace household," she said importantly. After saying, "Hi, Aunt Zoe," Helena rattled off a string of activities she had been doing at preschool. When Zoe was able to get a word in edgewise, she must have asked to talk to Kathy, because Helena thrust the portable phone at her.

"Hi, Zoe," Kathy said tentatively.

"Hi, kid. I thought Sunday was a good time to catch you there."

"We're just finishing breakfast."

"Well, I haven't forgotten about your weekend in New York," Zoe said. "My roommate is going out of town for Thanksgiving, and I remembered how much you *didn't* enjoy last year's family gathering. I thought maybe you'd like an alternative."

According to her parents' divorce agreement, Kathy was supposed to spend most of her holidays with Dr. Wallace and his family. This arrangement had met with varying degrees of success. Last Thanksgiving had been a low point.

"It sounds great," Kathy began, "but that Sunday is my birthday, and I was going to have a party with, uh . . ." she glanced over at Anne, "my friends from camp."

Her friends from Camp Wildwood actually had a name—the Holiday Five. Two summers ago, Kathy, Lia Greene, Jill Lewis, Maddy Donaldson, and Erin Moriarity had decided they would keep up their camp friendship even though they all lived in different places in and around Chicago. To do that, they got together on holidays, and now it was a tradition none of them wanted to break. Right from the first, Anne, who was a year older than Kathy, thought the concept was babyish and the name worse. There was usually a snide smile on her face when Kathy brought them up, just like there was now.

"That's right! Your thirteenth birthday. Welcome to the wonderful world of teenage angst," Zoe said. "Look, Kathy, the whole group of you are welcome if you can think of a way to swing it. Kick it around with Elliot and your mother and let me know. If you decide to come, try to be here by Thursday morning. You can see the Macy's Thanksgiving Day parade right from my window."

Zoe asked to talk to Marion next, and Kathy handed over the phone. Enthusiastically, she told her father about Zoe's invitation, glancing over at Anne every once in a while to make sure her stepsister was aware that Zoe told her to bring four friends and that she was invited for the whole holiday weekend.

But when Kathy mentioned the parade, Anne snorted. "Why doesn't she just ask Helena? Who else wants to see some overblown Snoopy being pulled through the streets?"

"There's something to be said for being young at heart, Anne," Dr. Wallace said mildly.

Fourteen-year-old Anne just made a face.

"You sound pretty excited about this, Kathy," her father continued.

"It would be great. Especially if I could go with my friends . . ." Kathy's voice trailed off. She didn't want to talk about this anymore. All of them going seemed like an incredible long shot. It probably wasn't even worth thinking about.

But on the way to the train station, Dr. Wallace brought up the trip again. "So, this New York thing sounds like fun."

Kathy looked at him warily. Didn't he care that she'd be gone for Thanksgiving? Usually, her father wanted nothing more than to try and wrap the Wallaces—steps, wholes, and halfs—into one tight holiday package. "You mean you think I should go?"

Dr. Wallace sighed. "Let's face it, my own special holiday five, you, Marion, Anne, Helena, and me, aren't as close as you and your friends. I know you don't much enjoy spending time with us."

"This summer wasn't bad," Kathy said.

"I agree, our trip to Europe worked out pretty well, but we were so busy seeing the sights, we didn't have to talk too much."

"By the time we got home after running around all day, we all just fell into bed." Kathy smiled slightly. "No time to argue."

"Look, thirteen is a special birthday. If you want to go to Zoe's, it's all right with me."

"Really? You'd let me go to Zoe's? You two never even got along that well."

"Don't get me started on that. If I think too much about giving you to scatterbrained Zoe for the weekend, I might change my mind."

"She's always been really nice to me."

"I know, I know. And now that she's moved to New York, I actually miss her . . . a little. If you want to go, Kathy, I'll even spring for the ticket as a birthday present."

"That would be great, Dad, but it wouldn't be as

much fun without the rest of the girls, and getting *that* together . . ."

Dr. Wallace nodded. "It was hard enough getting Erin to camp last summer."

Erin had originally gone to Camp Wildwood on a Family Services scholarship. Last summer, it had seemed that camp was impossible for her, until Kathy was able convince the camp owner to let Erin attend through a combination of scholarship and work.

"I can't see how the Moriaritys could come up with money for a plane ticket," Kathy said, "and it might be hard to convince the other parents anyway. It *is* Thanksgiving weekend after all."

Pulling into a parking space in front of the train station, Dr. Wallace said, "If anyone can pull it off, it's you, Princess. The way you handled Mrs. Tillman and that scholarship for Erin, I think you can do anything you put your mind to."

"Really?" Kathy said, pleased.

"Tell you what," Dr. Wallace said, giving Kathy a hug. "I'll even throw in one of my frequent flier tickets. And your Mom's friend Donna works at a travel agency. Maybe she knows about some cheap fares. Think about it."

Think about it was all Kathy did on the way home. Even though she saw a million problems with the idea, maybe more, she was pleased that her father had enough confidence in her to believe she could work them out. Could she? She supposed it might be fun to try.

The first thing Kathy did was talk to her mother. There was no point in going any further with the idea if her mother thought it was impossible. But Mrs. Wallace was surprisingly supportive.

"It's hard enough that your father gets you for most of the holidays," Kathy's mother said, as she fixed herself a cup of tea and Kathy some cocoa. "But what makes it worse is that you never seem to have a very good time."

"That's what Daddy said," Kathy murmured.

"Well, for once I agree with Elliot. This would be special, a special holiday and a special birthday. Let's see if we can arrange it. If all of your friends can't go, maybe one or two could make it."

"Oh, no," Kathy said. "I wouldn't feel right about leaving some of the girls behind."

Mrs. Wallace shook her head. "That will make it harder. But we'll give it a shot."

*   *   *

Later, after it was all accomplished, Kathy wondered if planning the military maneuvers for the Gulf
War had been any more complicated. That evening
Mrs. Wallace had called Zoe. They had never met, but
they had a pleasant conversation, and Mrs. Wallace
told Zoe she would keep her updated on all the
arrangements.

"She was very nice," Mrs. Wallace said after she'd
hung up the phone.

"I told you she was."

"She seems much more carefree than Marion."

That was an understatement, Kathy thought. Marion was Ms. Prim, while Zoe was practically a latter-
day hippie. Kathy thought she'd spare her mother that
particular insight.

The next day, Mrs. Wallace called her friend who
worked at the travel agency. Donna found some rea-
sonable airfares, and Mrs. Wallace agreed that she
would put in some of her frequent flier mileage along
with Dr. Wallace's to make the trip possible for at least
two of the girls besides Kathy.

That was the easy part. The complications really
began when Kathy tried to coordinate the weekend
with the rest of the girls.

All of the girls had been incredibly excited when Kathy called with the invitation.

"New York!" Lia had squealed. "I was there a couple of years ago, and I've wanted to go back ever since. Let me talk to my parents and call you right back."

Actually, Lia's call had come a couple of hours later and only after heavy negotiations with her parents.

"They finally said yes." Lia's birthday was coming up in December, and Mr. and Mrs. Greene agreed that, like Kathy, she could have a ticket to New York for her birthday present. "But my father has cousins in New York, and my parents want me to spend some time with them," Lia groaned.

"Do you have to?"

"Yeah, I think I do."

"So we'll fit it in. Who cares as long as you can go."

Maddy took a little more work. Maddy's mom, a widow, wasn't too crazy about the idea at first. Maddy was her only child, and they had never been apart for Thanksgiving. But Mrs. Donaldson was dating Lia's uncle, a romance that had been arranged by the girls. He had convinced Maddy's mother that "travel was broadening" and the trip was too good an experience to pass up. Finally she had agreed.

Jill's and Erin's presence was even tougher to arrange. Jill's parents didn't think it was fair to Jill's brother to send her on such an expensive trip. But when Mrs. Wallace called the Lewises and offered her a free ticket, they finally decided to let Jill go.

Erin was the most difficult. But before the usual question of finances arose, Kathy had told her about the second free ticket.

"Maybe my folks will say yes if I tell them I'll use my baby-sitting money to pay for everything else."

Kathy didn't hear from Erin for several days after that, but she didn't want to call and bug her.

Finally, an excited Erin telephoned.

"I can go!" she cried.

"That's great!" Kathy responded.

"I really had to do some talking. You know how holidays are around my house. Family and more family, and it was like no one was going to be able to swallow a bite of turkey if I wasn't there."

"So what changed their minds?"

"My sister Maureen got invited to spend the weekend with a friend of hers who moved to Indianapolis. Well, she wasn't about to let her trip get ruined, and my parents knew that if they let Maureen go, they couldn't say no to me."

"So they said yes," Kathy said happily.

"Yep. I have forty dollars in baby-sitting money saved," Erin said, a little anxiously. "Do you think that's enough?"

"More than enough," Kathy assured her. "We'll have most of our meals at Zoe's."

"I can't wait," Erin said. "We're going to have a great time."

"The best," Kathy agreed. "The absolute best."

TWO

"Hey, cool, our row has five seats," Erin said as the girls made their way down the aisle of the plane. "They must have known we were coming."

The Holiday Five stowed their bags and took their seats. Then Lia started laughing.

"What's so funny?" Maddy asked, a little grumpily. She had woken up with a sore throat yesterday morning, and it wasn't any better today, but she hadn't told her mother. There was no way she was going to miss this trip just because she was feeling under the weather.

"This is the only row on the whole plane that's full."

"I guess a six A.M. flight on Thanksgiving morning wasn't a hot ticket," Jill said.

"That's why we got such a good fare," Kathy said, mildly irritated. Since the flight left so early, there had been a sleepover at Kathy's Wednesday night. The girls had to get to the airport when it was still dark and very cold, and there had been plenty of groans about the early hour. True, getting up at four-thirty in the morning wasn't the most pleasant start to a day, but the way Kathy's friends had grumbled, you would have thought they were going to be shot at dawn, not boarding a flight for one of the most exciting cities in the world.

Maddy, shivering a little, put her coat over her like a blanket. "I'm going to sleep."

"But you'll miss the sunrise," Lia said.

"Wake me when they serve breakfast," Maddy replied, as she closed her eyes.

"How are you doing?" Jill asked Erin.

"What do you mean?"

"Well, this is the first time you've flown, right?"

"So?" Erin asked crossly. "Do you think I'm scared or something?" Erin could get mad fast. This time she was angry because Jill was getting a little too close to the truth. As excited as she had been when everything about the trip had fallen into place, a tiny little part of her had worried about flying. That part had spread like ooze until at this moment, she wished she had never agreed to go to New York at all.

How did these giant planes get up in the air, anyway? It didn't make any sense at all. A big chunk of metal, full of passengers and luggage, and it could just take off into the sky? And stay there? Erin knew in her head it happened all over the world thousands of times a day, but sitting here, strapped into her seat, it didn't seem logical—much less safe.

But Erin had a reputation for being not only feisty but fearless. She wasn't about to show her friends any fear of flying. "Why should I be afraid?" she finally answered Jill. "It doesn't bother the birds, does it?"

All the other girls laughed. And none of them noticed how tightly Erin gripped the arms of her seat when the plane finally did take off. To keep her mind off the fact that she was soaring through the air, Erin challenged Jill to a game of checkers. She had brought a little travel version of the game with magnetic pieces. Maddy promptly fell asleep. But Kathy and Lia spent most of the flight talking.

"Boy, we're going to be so close to Boston," Lia said as the flight attendant took away their breakfast trays. "It's too bad there's no way for you and Rick to get together."

Rick Weller had been an important part of Kathy's summer. He hadn't wanted to come to Camp Wildwood, but he had warmed up to the place once he had gotten together with Kathy. They had spent the whole summer together, and Kathy, who had never had a boyfriend before, had walked around feeling like she belonged on the cover of one of those romance paperbacks.

When camp was over, Kathy had gone on vacation with her father and his family, and Rick had moved with his family from Chicago to Boston. Things had stayed fine between them. At least at first.

"I haven't heard from Rick in at least a month," Kathy said flatly. "He doesn't even know I'm going to be on the East Coast."

"What happened?" Lia asked with surprise.

"We had a fight on the phone."

"You didn't say anything about it."

"I kept thinking he'd call back. And when he didn't I didn't want to think about him at all."

That sounded like Kathy, Lia thought to herself. "What did you fight about?" she asked tentatively.

"We were having an okay conversation. But Rick was slipping into one of his moods."

"Grouchy?"

Kathy nodded. "Like when he first came to camp. So, I was asking him if he was making friends, and out of the blue he said, 'Don't you want me to?'"

"And you said?" Lia prompted.

"I said, of course I wanted him to have friends. But Rick said, whenever he did talk about the few friends he was making, I started acting cold."

"Do you?"

Kathy shrugged. "I don't know. Maybe."

Lia, who had a definite practical streak, said, "Kathy, he does live halfway across the country. You don't want him to be lonely and miserable, do you?"

A part of Kathy wanted to say yes. Well, not miserable, but lonely enough to spend his free time thinking about her. That's what she did with her free time. She spent a lot of it just lying on her bed and moving back and forth between the past and the future.

Sometimes, she was at camp, and she remembered every one of what she'd come to call the Firsts. The first time Rick had held her hand. That happened almost by accident. There was a late-night splash party down at the lake for the older boys and girls. Kathy and Rick had been swimming and laughing and she'd swallowed a little bit of water and had stumbled out of the lake back to dry land. A concerned Rick had helped her out of the water, but then he hadn't let go of her hand.

The first kiss had come not long after that. Rick must have been planning it, because he'd seemed nervous all night. It had been a pretty ordinary evening—dinner in the dining hall, and then a talent show. Rick walked her halfway back to her cabin, which was really as close as the boys were supposed to get to the girls' cabins, but instead of saying good night like he usually did, he sort of pulled her into the shadows around a pine, shyly put his hand on her shoulder, and kissed her lightly on the mouth. It was over almost before Kathy realized what had happened. It was funny to think that something she had mulled over for hours and hours had lasted only seconds.

Then there was their first argument. It had been so stupid. The older kids had a dance with another nearby camp, and she had danced a couple of dances with a boy who had been at Wildwood last year. Rick had gotten jealous, she'd gotten mad, and they had had a fight, which Rick apologized for once he realized what an idiot he was being. As painful as it had been to have a fight with someone she liked so much, the first make-up was almost more exciting than the first kiss.

When she wasn't spending time remembering, she was daydreaming about the future. Kathy had never thought she had a particularly good imagination, but when it came to picturing herself going to the junior prom with Rick, or even their wedding, she was entranced for the longest time. It was usually her mother who'd find her staring out the window, and wake her with a sharp, "Kathy, come back to earth. You look like you're lost in space."

Now, on the plane, Lia said almost the same thing. "Where are you, Kathy?"

"Back at camp."

"So, you never finished your story. How did the fight start? Or end?"

Kathy shrugged. "I got mad, then he got mad. A couple of days later, I called back, but his mother answered, and I didn't leave my name."

"So he doesn't know you tried to get in touch?"

"I guess not. But he could have called me back. He didn't, so I guess he doesn't care anymore."

Lia felt bad for Kathy. She tried to change the subject. "Well, let's try not to think about him this weekend. We're here to have fun."

"That's right." Kathy's expression was determined. "We're going to have fun."

The flight was shorter than Erin had thought it would be, much to her relief. Nervously, she buckled her belt for the descent. If she could get through this part, everything would be just fine—until it was time to go home, anyway.

"I always hate landing," Jill confided as she buckled her own belt.

"You do? Why?"

"That big bump at the end."

Erin hadn't known about the big bump. Her heart pounding, she sat stiffly in her seat, gripping its arms, waiting for the bump. In the end it was more like a roll than a bump. "That wasn't so bad," she said accusingly to Jill.

"Some pilots are better than others." Jill shrugged as she put on her coat.

Erin didn't know whether she was relieved that the landing had been bumpless or mad that she'd worried all the way down for nothing.

To the girls' surprise, LaGuardia Airport, where they landed, was much smaller than Chicago's O'Hare.

"It's dinky!" Maddy said, looking around.

It was also pretty empty, and there was no Zoe in sight.

"Where's your aunt?" Jill asked a little nervously.

"She's always running late," Kathy said. Tardiness was one of Zoe's main characteristics, so Kathy wasn't too worried—yet.

"Maybe we should go down and get our luggage?" Lia suggested.

"No," Kathy said, "she told me we should wait by the gate. . . . Oh, there she is."

The girls turned in the direction Kathy was looking. Hurrying toward them was a woman in her early thirties swathed in a big plaid coat that resembled the sort of blanket Maddy would throw around a horse after riding it. Her hair was tucked under a red beret, and she wore red gloves that matched. She smiled at them and waved.

"Sorry we're late," Zoe said, huffing a little. "I can't even blame traffic. There wasn't any." Then she turned to an attractive man standing a little way behind her, as if he wasn't quite sure he wanted to be the only male in their circle. "This is my friend Hank Chavis." She gave Kathy a hug. "Hi, Birthday Girl. We're going to have so much fun."

After that, the girls were swept up in the whirlwind that was Zoe. She helped them get their luggage, and led them to the car, chattering all the way. Hank was either the strong, silent type or else he couldn't get a word in edgewise. Once though, he leaned over to Lia and whispered, "She'll calm down. At least, I hope she will." Lia just looked up at him, unable to think of a snappy comeback. Hank smiled at her and at that second, Lia had the strangest sensation, like she was falling down a hole or maybe being lifted back into the clouds she had just come out of. After that, she had trouble keeping her eyes off Hank, though she made a big effort to do so.

The ride home was a little crowded, but Hank had a good-sized car. Traffic was light on the way back, even when they got into the city.

"You should see it on a regular weekday," Zoe informed them. "Cars gridlocked, taxis flying over them, poor pedestrians trying to walk through them."

Kathy had been to New York with her mother, but except for Lia when she was nine, none of the other girls had ever visited the city. Even though they were used to Chicago, hardly a small town, New York was different. The buildings were taller and pressed together, there was more graffiti, more stores, more people—just more.

Hank sped through the east side of town over to the west, where Zoe's apartment was.

"Where are the houses?" Maddy asked with a frown.

"It's not like Chicago. No one in Manhattan lives in houses," Zoe responded. "It's all apartments, or townhouses if you're very rich. Houses are out in the suburbs."

"What's that?" Maddy asked, sitting up. There were barricades and a horde of people lining the streets, just a few blocks away.

"The parade," Zoe said.

"Oh, that's right, the Macy's Thanksgiving Day parade," Jill said.

"I'm going to let you off here," Hank said, "and bring the luggage over later. There's no way I'm going to be able to drive through this mess."

Zoe and the girls piled out of the car. Zoe said, "My apartment is just about the beginning of the parade route. There's a kind of holding pen there where the floats and the people wait until it's their turn to begin. Isn't it fun?"

Actually, Kathy thought, it looked as if they were walking into someone's bad dream. The kind you get when you've eaten too many sweets. Milling around the street were pilgrims, ballerinas, dancing flowers, big fat honeybees—and those were just the people in costume. Floating above them were familiar faces from cartoons blown up a thousand times their regular size, almost under the control of the people who were holding onto their ropes. Add many impressive floats and a dozen marching bands, and the whole thing seemed unreal, especially after just a couple of hours sleep.

Zoe tried to shepherd them across the streets through the police barricades, but it wasn't easy, especially when the girls kept stopping to look at things. Finally, they reached the lobby of Zoe's apartment building, and she let out a sigh. The girls followed her into the lobby, and she began introducing them to the doorman.

"James, this is my niece Kathy. She and her friends are going to be staying with me for a few days. We've got Maddy, Lia, Jill, and—" Zoe looked around, but the lobby was empty. "Oh, my gosh! Where's Erin?"

THREE

Erin strolled along trying to take it all in. She had been to parades before, especially the Saint Patrick's Day parade in Chicago, when the city dyed the river green. But she'd always been on the sidelines as the parade rolled by. To be here at the very starting point of the parade with floats and bands and people all mixing with one another was much more exciting.

"Hi."

Erin looked over at a boy about her age who was dressed like a junior member of the starship *Enterprise*. "Hi," she said. "Star Trek?"

The boy nodded. "It's that float over there." He

pointed to a bullet-shaped float with several Trekkies walking around on it.

"Have you ever been on the show?" Erin asked, impressed.

"Just an extra," he said nonchalantly.

"Wow."

Together, they examined the float a little more closely. Erin was beginning to feel that the glamour was rubbing off on her.

"What's your name?" Kevin asked.

Erin told him and then the boy introduced himself. "Kevin O'Rourke."

"You're Irish, too?"

"Sure am." Kevin said. "Do you live here?"

"No, I'm visiting." Erin clapped her hand over her mouth. "Oh no!"

"What's wrong?"

Looking around feverishly, Erin answered, "I must have gotten separated from the people I'm here with. I was so busy looking at the parade stuff . . ."

"Chill, Erin. Where were you going?"

"To an apartment building. Right around here, at least that's what Zoe said."

Kevin didn't even bother to ask who Zoe was. "Do you have the address?"

The address. She hadn't written it down, but she thought she remembered it. "Seventy-Fifth and Broadway, I think."

"Then you're not lost. It's either that apartment building," Kevin said, pointing to an imposing gray structure, "or that modern one across Seventy-Fifth Street."

"But how will I know which?"

"Just ask the doorman if Zoe lives there."

"Oh sure," Erin said with relief. But now it seemed that she wouldn't be roaming through the wilds of New York, she felt her relief mix with embarrassment. "You must think I'm an idiot."

"No, I think you're pretty cute."

Erin looked up, startled. She wasn't used to boys being quite this forward. It must be because Kevin was from New York. "Well, I'd better get going. Everyone's gotta be worried about me."

"Will I see you again?" Kevin asked.

"Zoe's apartment overlooks the parade route. I'll wave to you."

"No, listen," Kevin said a little urgently—a man in a suit was rounding up all the Trekkies—"I know today is Thanksgiving and all, but what about tomorrow?"

"I told you, I'm just visiting with my friends," Erin

said helplessly. "We're all going to do stuff together."

"Tomorrow, in the afternoon, I'm going to be skating at Rockefeller Center."

"Where's that?"

Kevin had to hurry; the man was waving him aboard the float, "Anyone will tell you. If you can, be there around one, okay?"

Erin just had time to nod as Kevin climbed aboard his spaceship. She doubted she'd ever see him again, but the encounter had been fun. If you didn't count the getting lost part.

Thankfully, the first building she tried, the staid gray stone, was Zoe's. She didn't even have to question the doorman, because as soon as she walked in he frowned and said, "Erin?"

"How did you know?"

"Ms. Hamilton is very worried about you. Go right up to 1013. She and your friends are waiting."

The doorman must have called ahead, because Zoe flung open the door before Erin even knocked.

"Thank goodness you're all right," she said, giving Erin a small hug.

"I'm sorry," Erin said, as Zoe led her into the apartment. "I turned around and you were all gone."

"You must have been walking really slow," Lia said.

"It's all right now," Zoe said. "I was just about to go downstairs and look for you."

"How did you find us?" Jill demanded.

"Oh, I remembered the address, and someone in the parade helped me," Erin said vaguely.

"Your first adventure in New York," Zoe said. "Well, now that you're here we can all relax and watch the end of the parade."

As she took off her coat, Erin looked around the apartment. It wasn't small like the Chicago apartments she had been in. Actually, it was rather luxurious. Erin immediately noticed the high ceilings, which made the living room feel spacious, and she could see down the long stretch of hallway that there were several bedrooms in the place. One wall of the living room was almost all windows, and that's where the girls were huddled. Erin could hear the noise of the parade coming from ten floors below.

"You scared us, Erin," Kathy said as Erin joined the girls at the window.

"We kept looking outside trying to see you," Lia added.

"But you didn't, right?" Erin was hoping they hadn't seen her standing around chatting with Kevin.

"No," Lia said. Then she looked at her curiously.
"Why?"

"Oh, I just didn't want you to see me wandering around like an idiot." The excuse sounded lame even to her own ears, but she didn't feel like talking about Kevin right this second. He was so cute. She wondered if she would ever see him again. An idea started to form in her mind.

Although they had missed a lot of the parade, there was still an hour or so left to watch. The girls helped Zoe make hot chocolate and they took turns hanging out the windows watching all the floats go by.

Maddy didn't pay too much attention. She wanted nothing so much as to lie down and take a nap, but it seemed rude to ask where the bedroom was. The hot chocolate felt good going down her raspy throat, so she had several cupfuls.

Lia noticed as Maddy topped her third cup with whipped cream. "You'd better be careful," Lia whispered to her. "We've got a lot of food to eat this weekend."

"What do you mean?" Maddy snapped.

Lia was surprised. Maddy was usually so easygoing. "It's just that your diet has been going so well."

It was true. Maddy had lost about fifteen pounds in the last nine months or so, just by watching what she ate and exercising more. Camp had been great for that. The food wasn't very good, and she was always riding and swimming. But though she was proud of her accomplishment, she didn't feel like watching herself every second. Especially not on Thanksgiving. Especially when she was feeling so lousy. "What are you? The food police?" Maddy asked Lia bitterly.

Kathy was walking toward the kitchen and heard what Maddy said. "Maddy!"

"How come I'm the only one whose every bite gets stared at?" Maddy complained.

Lia and Kathy exchanged glances. "I was only trying to help," Lia finally said.

"Okay, but just don't bug me. We've got a big Thanksgiving dinner coming up. I'd like to enjoy it."

Kathy called over to Zoe, who was leaning out the window watching the parade. "Do you need any help with dinner, Zoe?"

Zoe shook her head. "I'll get to it in a while."

"Have you put the turkey in yet?"

"No. We're not going to eat until four or so. It's only a quarter to eleven." She turned back to the parade.

Lia whispered to Kathy. "Hey, I'm no expert, but depending how big the turkey is, it should be in the oven soon."

Kathy shrugged. "I'm sure Zoe will get into cooking when the parade is done."

But after the last float had passed by, Zoe showed them around the apartment and got them settled. Then the girls, whose lack of sleep was catching up with them, asked if they could take a nap before dinner.

"I guess so," Zoe responded. She looked at her watch. "Gee, I'd better get to the turkey." So while Maddy, Lia, Jill, and Erin settled in for a nap, Kathy followed Zoe out to the kitchen.

"Aren't you tired?" Zoe asked.

"I'm past tired. I'll help you for a while."

Zoe went to the refrigerator and took out the biggest turkey Kathy had ever seen.

"It's huge!" Kathy said.

"A twenty pounder," Zoe said proudly, as if she had raised it herself.

"But we didn't need anything that big."

"We didn't?" Zoe looked critically at the turkey. "I've never made one of these before. With Hank, we're going to be seven people. And then, we'll want leftovers. I thought I should get something good sized."

"You sure did. How long will it take to cook?"

Zoe put on her glasses and read the cooking instructions. "It says twenty-five minutes per pound."

Silently, Kathy and Zoe did the math.

"I guess I should have started it earlier," Zoe said, looking a little worried.

"It'll take hours and hours."

"Well, I'll put it in right now. And I'll turn it up high. Maybe it will cook faster. And I won't stuff it. That'll save time."

Kathy didn't want to say that the stuffing was the best part. Hurriedly, Zoe put the turkey in an aluminum roasting pan and started it cooking. "There. Now I'll do the side dishes."

While Kathy chopped vegetables, Zoe threw some sweet potatoes into a large pot. "What do you do with these when they're cooked?" Zoe asked.

Kathy thought about it. "My mother mixes up orange juice and brown sugar, I think, and then dribbles it on."

"We don't have either."

"I guess we can just put butter on them."

"Okay," Zoe said agreeably.

"What else are you serving?" Kathy asked.

"I bought olives."

"Olives are good."

"Salad. And those brown-and-serve rolls. And that's it."

Kathy thought dinner sounded a little skimpy, especially without the stuffing, but since Zoe was being nice enough to make dinner, Kathy didn't feel it would be appropriate to complain. She did, however, say, "What about dessert?"

Zoe clapped her hand to her mouth. "Oops. I was going to get some pumpkin pie. I forgot."

"Is it too late to get something now?"

"I'll call Hank. He's watching a football game. I'll tell him to pick something up on the way over."

Kathy wondered if she should suggest that Hank pick up a main course, too. She had serious doubts about that turkey.

In the back bedroom, which was used as a den, Erin was trying to get comfortable on the Hide-A-Bed she was sharing with Jill. Maddy and Lia were bunking in Zoe's roommate's bedroom. "So, Jill," Erin said in what she hoped was a casual tone. "What do you know about Rockefeller Center?"

"I think that's where they have a big Christmas tree. And there's an ice-skating rink there."

"A skating rink. I bet you'd really like to see that."

"I guess."

"I would, too. Maybe we could ask Zoe if we could go tomorrow."

Jill, who was plumping her pillow, stopped and looked at Erin curiously. "What's up, Erin?"

"What do you mean?"

"C'mon. You've never shown that much interest in skating. Now you're interested in a skating rink?"

Erin flopped back against her own pillow. "All right, all right, I met a boy."

"When?" Jill asked, startled.

"When I was trying to find my way here."

Jill whistled. "You are fast, girl. But you shouldn't have been talking to strange boys."

"He was in the parade. He asked me to meet him tomorrow at the ice-skating rink at Rockefeller Center."

"How old was he?"

"He was our age. And he was really cute," Erin told her. "It was—I don't know—exciting, the way he asked me to meet him."

Jill looked at Erin skeptically. "But what good will meeting him there do? I mean, you'll never get to see him after that."

"It would just be romantic," Erin said. "Don't you think?"

"Not particularly." Jill was a practical sort. "But I do want to see Rockefeller Center, so I guess there's no harm in asking if we can go."

"In the afternoon. That's when he's going to be there."

"Okay, okay, I'll ask Zoe if we can visit Rockefeller Center. In the afternoon. I'm closing my eyes now. All right?"

Erin smiled her thanks. "Sweet dreams."

When the girls opened their eyes, about four hours later, it was almost dark. Jill sat up. "I think I smell the turkey cooking."

But in the kitchen, Zoe was looking worriedly in the oven. "Do you think it looks done?" she asked Kathy.

"It's brown," Kathy said uncertainly. "But that pop-up thing hasn't popped up yet."

Zoe and Kathy's gazing was interrupted by a banging at the door.

"I'll get it," Kathy said, anxious to get away from the turkey.

"Hey there," Hank said, as he tried to balance the girls' luggage he was bringing up from his car. "Is dinner ready? I'm starved."

"We're not sure," Kathy said.

Lia, who had gotten up a few minutes earlier, came

into the hallway. "Can I help you with that stuff?" she asked shyly.

Hank dropped the bags and gave her a smile. "Best offer I've had all day."

Lia felt her heart do a little tap dance. Zoe was so lucky. Hank was almost movie-star handsome, and he was so nice. Just being this close to him made her feel nervous and happy at the same time. She wasn't sure if she wanted to engage him in conversation or run away and watch television.

But Hank seemed to want to talk to her. "So what did you do today?" he asked conversationally as they brought her bag and Maddy's quietly into the room where Maddy was still sleeping.

Lia pointed her finger at Maddy. "That's all."

"You needed the sleep, I guess, but tomorrow you'll see more of New York."

Jill and Erin were already up and about when Hank and Lia brought them their bags.

"Is it time for dinner?" Jill asked.

"I hope so," Hank replied. "Let's see what's happening in the kitchen.

In the kitchen, a flustered Zoe was poking around the turkey. Everyone else was in there too, except

Maddy. "It's not done yet," she said. "I hope you're not too hungry."

Everyone murmured, "No, no," or "That's all right." No one said, "I'm starving!" which is what they all were thinking.

If they were starving then, they were famished two hours later when Zoe finally put the turkey on the table. "Well," she said uncertainly. "There it is."

It looked a little odd. It was brown, but not brown all over. Some parts seemed decidedly pale. There were also lots of puncture holes and slices hacked off the top of the turkey where Zoe had made inroads to see if it was done. It gave the turkey a wounded look.

"Why don't we start with the salad," Hank suggested, "while I carve the turkey."

"Okay," Zoe said.

The dinner that followed was like no other Thanksgiving that any of the girls had experienced. While they dutifully ate their salad, they watched Hank try to carve a turkey that didn't seem to want to be carved.

"Is it done?" Zoe kept asking nervously.

"Well, it's not pink. That's good," he replied optimistically. Then he added, "But parts of it look a little burned."

"How could that be?" Lia whispered to Kathy. "I thought you were worried it hadn't cooked long enough."

"Maybe it's because she turned the heat up so high."

After Kathy and Erin helped clear the salad plates, the turkey was served, along with the sweet potatoes, the rolls, and, of course, the olives.

Far and away, the olives were the most popular part of the meal. Zoe had found some brown sugar at the back of the cupboard to sprinkle on the sweet potatoes, but without the orange juice to cut the sugar, the potatoes were way too sweet. The brown-and-serve rolls were all right, but a little too brown.

As for the turkey, well, none of the girls had ever tasted turkey quite like it. There were bites that had a smoky bitter taste and others that tasted like plastic, and occasionally, but only occasionally, there was a bite that was absolutely normal.

Everyone chewed quietly. Into the silence, Zoe dropped her fork loudly against the china plate. "It's awful, I know. You don't have to eat anymore." She got up and began taking the dishes away, even though some of the girls were in mid-bite.

"Zoe, it's fine," Erin said.

"The salad was great," Maddy added, then noticed Kathy sending her a frown. "Because I'm on a diet," Maddy continued hurriedly. "So it's great not to have all that food you usually have at Thanksgiving . . ." Her voice dribbled away.

"You're all trying to be nice," Zoe said, her own voice trembling a little. "But it's awful. I thought it would be easier . . ."

"All right, all right," Hank said, getting up. "The turkey didn't work out. But that doesn't mean we're going to starve. We've had our salads, and our olives. What else do you have in the fridge?" he asked Zoe.

She sniffed and shrugged.

"Cheese?" Hank asked. When Zoe nodded, he said, "Bread?"

"I think so."

He put his arm around her and gave her a hug. "Let's go see. Kids, we'll be right back."

"Wow," Lia said as she watched them go into the kitchen.

"Wow that we're going to have grilled cheese sandwiches for Thanksgiving dinner?" Jill wanted to know.

"No," Lia said scornfully. "Wow, what a guy."

FOUR

Kathy felt two things when she got up. Grumpy and hungry. Or maybe she was grumpy because she was hungry. The grilled cheese sandwich last night had filled her up, but just barely. Normally, it would have been plenty; she had had just a sandwich for dinner many times. But that was always by choice. Thanksgiving was supposed to be something special, and she had missed the festive holiday air as much as the actual food. Perhaps that's what she was really hungry for.

Zoe was still sleeping, so Kathy tried to be quiet as she made her way to the bathroom. As a rule, she woke up in a good mood. But this morning, it was as if a black cloud was over her head. She wondered if

everyone was mad at her because Thanksgiving dinner had been such a disappointment. They had certainly been quiet when they went to bed. Then *she* got
mad. It wasn't her fault Zoe was a bad cook. Besides,
the girls wouldn't even be in New York if it wasn't for
her. They'd better not be angry, Kathy thought as she
brushed her teeth.

By the time Kathy had showered and got dressed,
Lia was already in the kitchen, making herself some
toast and hot chocolate.

"Want some?" she asked Kathy.

"I guess."

"What's with you?" One didn't have to be particularly sensitive to catch Kathy's mood.

"I suppose everyone is angry about dinner last
night," she said, taking the cup of hot chocolate that
Lia handed her.

"No. Not really. I mean, Zoe is a little scatterbrained, but she's been really nice to us."

"Yes, she has," Kathy responded, glad that Lia was
aware of it. "But no one seemed to be having a very
good time last night."

"Oh Kathy, we were all tired. We can't get mad over
a little burned turkey."

Finally, a smile twitched the corners of Kathy's mouth. "To say nothing of the sweet potato frosting."

The girls giggled softly. "I don't think I've ever tasted anything quite like that sweet potato side dish. Instant cavities," Lia said. "It's a good thing my uncle is a dentist."

Maddy, who was feeling a little better this morning, joined them. "I guess you didn't have to worry about me eating too many calories last night," she said, grabbing some milk from the refrigerator.

"We were just talking about dinner," Lia said.

"I felt sorry for Zoe. Maybe we should do something nice for her today."

"That would be good," Kathy agreed.

"Of course, it wasn't her fault we didn't get any pumpkin pie," Maddy reminded them.

That had been another disappointment. After the girls had polished off their grilled cheese sandwiches, they had been looking forward to at least having the pie. But Hank had had so much to carry with their bags and all, he'd forgotten the pie and whipped cream on his kitchen table. He had run down to a twenty-four-hour market and gotten some ice cream, but it hadn't been the same.

"No wonder he forgot," Lia said. "His arms were full of our stuff."

Erin and Jill walked in on Lia's defense of Hank. "I bet that's not all you wished his arms were full of," Jill teased.

Lia started to blush. "You're being ridiculous." Last night, the girls had noticed the stars in Lia's eyes when she'd mentioned Hank's gallantry, and they'd given her the business until it was time to go to bed.

"What would Scott think if he knew how you felt about Hank?" Erin asked, mentioning the boy Lia liked.

"You mean would he be jealous? Hank is probably twenty years older than me."

"You were really impressed with the way he treated Zoe last night," Kathy reminded her.

"He was very nice," Lia agreed. "What was the big deal about mentioning it?" Not for the world would she let even these good friends know how being around Hank was affecting her. She had never really had a crush on anyone before. She liked Scott a lot, but he was as much a best friend as a boyfriend. Hank was totally out of her league, but her heart—and stomach—did a little flip-flop when he walked by. And somersaulted when he spoke to her.

"Who was nice?" Zoe asked, as she came into the kitchen, rubbing her eyes.

The girls just looked at each other, but Lia boldly said, "Hank. The way he took care of everything after the dinner . . ." Lia didn't know what to say that would still sound polite.

"Flopped," Zoe finished for her, as she put on the coffee. "I'm really sorry, girls. We'll order pizza tonight."

That sounded safe enough, Kathy thought.

"So what are we going to do today?" Erin asked in what she hoped was a casual tone.

"Well, I thought we'd go sightseeing," Zoe responded. "Any special requests?"

Erin gave Jill a small kick.

"How about Rockefeller Center?" Jill said, unobtrusively kicking Erin right back.

Zoe sipped her coffee. "Oh, sure. That's a must. It's a little cold for the Statue of Liberty today, but there are plenty of other things to see. Why don't we take the subway down to the Empire State Building, then hit Rockefeller Center, and walk up Fifth Avenue after that. Let's get dressed and get going."

Erin glanced up at the kitchen clock. It was only nine-thirty. Way too early to get to Rockefeller Center if seeing Kevin was the object. "You want to get to Rockefeller Center about eleven then?" Erin asked.

"Why not?" Kathy looked at her curiously.

"Isn't there anything around here to see?"

Zoe laughed. "Of course there is. We can walk through the park and down to Fifth Avenue, if you prefer. I forget to tell you it's going to be really crowded," Zoe warned. "This is the busiest shopping day of the year, you know."

"I think that sounds like fun," Jill said.

Zoe just laughed. "Okay, if it's not too cold we'll just start up here and walk down to Fifth, then to Rockefeller Center, and wind up at the Empire State Building. After that, we'll see what we want to do next."

Erin did some calculations in her head. Maybe if they walked slowly enough and stopped at enough places along the way, they might get to Rockefeller Center about the right time.

She certainly did her best to drag things out. She was the last to finish dressing, causing Kathy to say crossly, "Come on, Erin, you're holding everything up." Once outside, Erin made sure to stop and look very carefully at everything Zoe pointed out.

"Aren't there any museums around?" Erin asked.

"The Metropolitan Museum is on the other side of the park."

"I'm dying to go there," Kathy said. "They have a wonderful fashion collection."

"We should go tomorrow," Zoe said. "When we can spend more time."

Actually, the museum sounded rather boring to Erin, but at least this morning it would have been a time waster. Tomorrow it wouldn't do her a bit of good.

Zoe suggested that they take a bus down to fashionable Fifth Avenue, but Erin wanted to walk, and to her surprise, the other girls agreed with her.

"It's not that cold when you keep moving," Jill said, "and there's so much to see."

So they walked along the park people-watching until they got to the end, where Maddy, who was beginning to feel draggy again, perked up when she saw the horse-drawn carriages that gave people rides around the park.

She walked right up to a particularly handsome horse with a paper rose in his bridle. "What's his name?" Maddy asked the carriage driver, a young man in a cape and top hat.

"Beauty."

"You're kidding! I ride a horse named Beauty at camp."

"You should take a ride around the park with this one."

Maddy looked hopefully at Zoe.

"These rides are very expensive," Zoe said, frowning.

"I'll give you a good rate since there are so many of you," the carriage driver said.

"I have some money. I'd love a ride," Erin piped up.

In the end, they decided on a short ride for a reduced rate, with the five girls going and Zoe running into one of the stores to do a little shopping. It was the most fun that they had had since arriving in New York. Kathy began to relax a little. She realized how responsible she'd been feeling for the other girls' having a good time.

Squished together in the open cab of the carriage, with blankets around their knees, they laughed as they rode around the park.

"I feel like the queen of England," Lia said. "She has a coach like this."

Jill waved to some of her imagined subjects. A couple of them waved back.

When they got out of the carriage, they had the driver

take a picture of them, with the camera Maddy had brought along, as they stood in front of the carriage. Zoe was already waiting for them, a gold shopping bag in her hand.

"What's that?" Erin asked.

"Beautiful wrapping paper," Zoe said, a smile playing around her lips.

As the girls continued their walk down Fifth Avenue, Jill whispered to Erin, "Have you bought anything for Kathy's birthday?"

Erin shook her head. "I thought I'd get something here." Then she asked the same question to Maddy and Lia, who were walking behind her.

They must have thought that Kathy was still back at the Tiffany window, where Zoe had stopped to look at some very beautiful jewelry. But Kathy had wandered up toward the group. She was close enough to hear them all say that they hadn't bought anything for her birthday.

"My mom made me buy her a necklace, but I'm not crazy about it," Lia said.

Maddy, who was starting to feel sick again, said, "Hey, we're in a big city. We can get anything, we don't have to do anything about it now."

Kathy turned away. Anything? How nice of her

friends to put so much thought into her present. She'd better tell Zoe to walk by the souvenir shops on Sixth Avenue. Maybe the girls could pick up a keychain that said I LOVE NEW YORK on it.

Zoe walked up to her. "I'm sorry I'm holding you up. I'm just crazy for Tiffany."

"It's great," Kathy said curtly.

"Are you okay?" Zoe asked with concern.

Kathy wouldn't have minded confiding in Zoe, but it didn't seem right to burden her. She had enough on her mind, shepherding five girls around New York. "Fine. Just a little tired."

"Well, you don't have time to be tired now. We've got a lot more to see."

Erin didn't have to try too hard to make their walk last longer. The streets were packed with day-after-Thanksgiving shoppers, making it hard to move. Besides, all the girls wanted to stop somewhere along the way, at a store window or to take a picture in front of St. Patrick's Cathedral. By the time they got to Rockefeller Center, it was a little before one, but not too much before. There was certainly a good chance that Kevin was there. If not, he'd probably be there soon.

"This place is awesome," Lia said, looking around.

"I'll say," Jill agreed. "Look at that Christmas tree. Have you ever seen a bigger one in your life?"

Maddy, who was exhausted by the trek down Fifth Avenue, said, "Can we rest here for a while?"

Erin almost kissed her. Maddy couldn't have made a better suggestion if she was in on the plan.

"Sure," Zoe said. "We can stop and have a light lunch at the restaurant that overlooks the rink. We're probably going to have to stand in line, though," Zoe warned. "This place is crawling with tourists."

"Jill, don't you want to see the rink?" Erin asked.

"I can see it."

"I mean close up." Erin's eyes implored Jill to say yes.

Jill didn't like being put in the middle of this deception, but she wouldn't mind seeing the rink, so she nodded.

"I don't see how we can refuse to let a real-life skater go down and look at the Rockefeller Center rink," Zoe said with a smile. "We'll go wait in line, and you come back after you've had a look around."

"I'll go with her," Erin said quickly.

"Anybody else?" Zoe asked.

To Erin's relief, the rest of the girls wanted to get inside and warm up for a few minutes. As they were walking down the stairs to the rink, Jill muttered, "We shouldn't be lying to Zoe. This isn't right."

"We're not really lying. You did want to go down and see the rink, didn't you?"

"Sure, but—"

"Oh, there he is," Erin said, trying not to sound too excited.

"Which one?"

"The boy with the red stocking cap on. Skating over there."

"His form isn't too bad," Jill commented.

Kevin spotted them and skated over. "Hey, you made it," he said, his eyes lighting up. Out of his Star Trek outfit, Kevin was even cuter today than he had been yesterday.

"Yes, but I can't stay too long. We're having lunch. Everyone else is waiting in line. This my friend Jill. She's a real skater. She's won prizes."

"You can rent skates here," Kevin informed her with a grin.

"No time." Jill smiled back at him. She had to admit, Kevin did seem nice.

"How was the parade?" Erin asked.

"Great. A float is a very cool place to watch the city go by."

"It must be great to live in a city like this." Jill said.

"Well, sure."

"We're getting the grand tour this morning," Erin told him. "But we're probably hitting all the tourist spots. You must know lots of great places tourists never get to see."

"We *are* tourists," Jill reminded Erin.

"You should let me show you around," Kevin said. "On the Kevin O'Rourke tour, you'd see things that are way off the beaten track." He looked down at Erin. "I'm free tomorrow. How about it? Want to go sight-seeing?"

FIVE

Erin looked back over her shoulder to wave once more at Kevin, but he had already skated off.

"You can't go," Jill insisted for the third time. The first time was right after Kevin made his offer to show Erin—and the offer seemed to be directed only at Erin—around the city. The second time came after Kevin gave Erin instructions about where they could meet tomorrow afternoon. Jill had tried not to sound pushy. She'd merely said, "Erin, I'm sure Zoe's made plans, so you probably can't go." Erin had just sort of shrugged and taken down the information about meeting Kevin at the Tower Records store on Broadway.

Now Jill was getting mad. "Erin, you can't just go running around New York with a boy you don't know."

"I'm not sure I'm going to do it," Erin said vaguely.

"You're all set up to meet at Tower Records."

"I didn't think I should just rule it out." What Erin didn't tell Jill was that meeting Kevin was one of the most exciting things that had ever happened to her. Cal, the boy she liked at camp, was sweet enough, but not very exciting. This was different. A really cute boy, a boy who had been on television no less, had picked her out of millions—literally millions!—to show around New York. Sure, she knew the odds of actually arranging things so she could see the city with Kevin were small, but it was thrilling just to be asked. Today, at least, she could pretend that she and Kevin were going out on a date. That is, she'd be able to pretend if Jill didn't keep telling her that she couldn't go.

"Are you going to tell the others?" Jill asked pointedly.

Erin shook her head. It seemed a little late for that now. "I didn't say anything yesterday, so I don't know how I'd explain it."

"Zoe would probably be mad if she found out that's why you lost us yesterday," Jill agreed.

Erin looked back over her shoulder once more. She could just see Kevin skating on the far side of the rink. "I got lost first," Erin said distractedly. "I wonder exactly what Zoe does have planned for tomorrow after-noon."

"Erin!"

Erin came back to earth. "Don't get upset," she told Jill. "You're right. I probably shouldn't even be think-ing about this." But she couldn't help it. It was hard to get Kevin off her mind.

By the time Erin and Jill rejoined the rest of their group, the other girls and Zoe were near the front of the line.

"Oh, it's a good thing you're back," Zoe said. "They weren't going to seat us unless everyone was here."

"Where were you anyway?" Kathy wanted to know. "You took an awfully long time just to check out a patch of ice."

There was an awkward silence until Erin said, "Jill got into it. Checking out the competition, I guess."

Jill glared at Erin. Her look clearly said, *Don't put me in the middle of this.*

Erin shrugged apologetically. Fortunately, the host-ess was showing them to their table, and no one else seemed to notice.

Following lunch, the girls took their first subway ride, down to Greenwich Village. Even though they lived in and around Chicago, of all the girls only Erin had a real familiarity with subways. Lia expected to be nervous riding the train, but although there were a couple of weirdos around, most of the passengers just seemed like people who had a destination.

Later, the girls agreed that the Village was one of their favorite parts of the trip. It looked very different from noisy midtown, and even from the residential area where Zoe lived. Here the streets were narrow and the buildings were much smaller. The sky wasn't filled with skyscrapers, the way so much of Manhattan was. It seemed much cozier.

The girls did some shopping, but Kathy couldn't tell if any of the things they bought were for her. She was still hurt about how casual everyone seemed to be about her birthday.

As the afternoon shadows were lengthening, Maddy said, "Are we going home soon?" She had been feeling better at the start of the day, but now, after a whole, long day of sight-seeing, she couldn't remember ever feeling worse. Her head was hot, her throat was scratchy, and she had serious doubts about making it home, wherever that was. She'd pretty much lost track of where they were in relation to Zoe's apartment.

"But there's that one store over there we said we'd

stop at on the way back—" Jill hadn't even finished her sentence when Maddy snapped, "You've already seen a hundred stores, maybe a thousand. You'll see more tomorrow. Can't we just go home?"

There was a surprised silence, then Lia said, "Someone's getting cranky."

The word *cranky* rattled around in Maddy's head for a second or two. She felt like she was going to keel over and die, and Lia called it "cranky"?

"I am not cranky." Maddy spit out the word. "I'm sick!"

Zoe may not have been a mom, but she knew how to act like one. In a second, she had her glove off and was feeling Maddy's forehead. "Wow, you're really hot."

Jill put her hand against Maddy's forehead. "Burning," she agreed.

Maddy pulled her head away. "Don't. I just want to go home." At that very second, she really did mean home, as in Waukegan home, but that seemed so far away from Greenwich Village it might be in another universe. She supposed she'd settle for Zoe's.

"Can you make it on the subway?" Zoe asked.

Maddy turned a bilious green at the thought.

"A cab's going to be a fortune," Zoe murmured to herself, "and probably not all that much faster. Still,

Maddy will be more comfortable in a cab." She turned to Kathy. "You go home with her in a taxi. I'll take the others on the subway."

Kathy looked at Zoe with dismay. Why was she going to get stuck with Maddy? And she didn't know her way around New York practically at all. What if the cab driver took her the wrong way and ran up a huge fare?

Zoe must have read her mind. "You ride taxis at home a lot. You know they're safe. And I gave you a key to the apartment." She looked at the other girls. "It's too easy to get mixed up on the subway. I've got to go with the others. So you go and we'll be right behind you. With this after-Thanksgiving shopping, we may even beat you uptown." She took a twenty-dollar bill out of her purse and gave it to Kathy for the fare.

It was hard not to feel sorry for Maddy. She really did look pathetic, pale one moment, flushed the next. "I'll take care of her," Kathy said with resignation.

Zoe put Kathy and Maddy into a taxi and gave the driver the address. Then the cab zoomed off.

"Oh," Maddy groaned, as the cab jerked in and out of traffic.

"What's wrong with her?" the cab driver asked, looking in the rearview mirror.

"She's sick," Kathy replied curtly.

"She's not going to throw up, is she?"

"I certainly hope not." Then she whispered to Maddy, "Are you?"

"No, it's not that kind of sick."

Well, that was something to be thankful for, Kathy thought. As she leaned back in the taxi and watched the buildings go by, she had to admit that she was feeling pretty sorry for herself. Even though Zoe was trying very hard, and though they had seen a lot of terrific things, this wasn't the way she had envisioned the weekend at all.

For one thing, she had expected her friends to make a bigger deal about the reason they were in New York—her birthday. Everyone was acting like they just happened to be having an exciting weekend in the most exciting city in the world. No one had really said thank you or even mentioned her birthday, except for the casual assertion that they could buy her anything.

Besides, everything seemed to be going wrong. If it wasn't the Thanksgiving dinner, it was Maddy getting sick. And there was one more nagging item that was ruining the weekend. Even though she and Rick were on the outs, she had thought he might use her birthday as an excuse to make up. But when she had called home last night and asked if she'd received any calls, her mother had replied, "No."

Her birthday wasn't actually until Sunday, so there was still a chance that she'd get a call. However, the way things were going, she probably shouldn't get her hopes up.

Maddy had fallen asleep on the ride home, and Kathy had to rouse her when they arrived at Zoe's house. Zoe's prediction notwithstanding, Kathy and Maddy arrived first, and Maddy had already climbed into her pajamas by the time Zoe and the others got back.

Zoe took Maddy's temperature and gave her a couple of Tylenol. Then she sent her right to bed.

She flopped down on the living-room couch after she had played nurse. "Do you think I should call her parents?" she asked the girls, who were watching television.

"How high was her temperature?" the practical Lia asked.

"Just about a hundred."

"Maybe she'll feel better when she gets up," Jill said optimistically.

"We're going to have pizza for dinner," Kathy said,

coming in from the kitchen. "If the smell of that doesn't make her feel better, then we'll start to worry."

Kathy's joke fell flat.

"That's kind of mean," Lia said.

"You rode home with her. You know how sick she is," Jill added.

Kathy was embarrassed, but she didn't want to show it. Instead, she answered flippantly, "She's not on her death bed. And I was just kidding around."

No one said anything, so Kathy stalked out of the room. She went into Zoe's room, and though she would have liked to slam the door, she merely closed it. Fine, she thought, if everyone thought she was being cruel, she would just stay out of the way. She grabbed a book from her knapsack and started to read. Maybe she would come out when Zoe ordered the pizza, maybe she wouldn't.

An hour later the pizza arrived. Even for pizza, Maddy didn't get out of bed, but she did eat the soup Zoe brought up from the deli. Kathy was starving, so she came out of the bedroom, but she was grateful when Zoe suggested they eat in front of the TV. One of the girls' favorite shows was on, and soon everyone began commenting on the hairdos and the fashions, and of course, the guys. Pretty soon, the tension had cleared.

As they were cleaning up, Lia said, "I'd better call my relatives. They're expecting to hear from me."

"Go ahead," Zoe said. "We can manage in here."

Lia went into the guest room and picked up the phone. She pulled her cousin Sylvia's number out of her jeans pocket and dialed.

"Hello, Sylvia?"

"Lia, is that you? Your mother called and said you'd be getting in touch."

"Yes. I'm here in New York."

"I'm glad to hear from you. Are you having a good time?"

Now there was a question. Was she? She'd certainly enjoyed all the sight-seeing she'd done in New York, but she didn't like the strange vibes that were flying around. Kathy was peeved, Erin was acting weird, Jill seemed distracted, and of course, Maddy was sick. "New York is great," she said carefully.

"I hope you've set aside some time to see us."

Lia didn't know her father's cousin very well, and she had been hoping that perhaps she'd be too busy to see Lia. But apparently not.

"We can meet for lunch tomorrow. My husband will be busy, but I'll bring the children."

Sylvia's children were five and seven. This wasn't sounding like fun. "I'm not sure what Kathy's aunt has planned . . ."

"Oh now, none of that. I'm sure your friends would excuse you for one afternoon."

"Well, let me talk to them, and I'll get back to you."

"Fine. Call me later."

Lia went into the kitchen. Since they'd used paper plates for the pizza, most of the work had already been done.

"Good timing," Jill said.

Lia looked at Jill. She seemed to be kidding, but who could tell for sure?

"My cousin Sylvia wants me to go out to lunch tomorrow. Will that be all right?" she asked Zoe.

Zoe nodded. "I don't see why not. Just make sure you're home in plenty of time to get to the theater."

As a special treat, Dr. Wallace had asked Zoe to purchase tickets for *Cats*, a long-running Broadway musical.

"I've seen the pictures of all those actors and actresses dressed up like cats, but what's the play about?" Erin asked.

"There's not really a story," Zoe told her. "The lyrics of all the songs are based on T. S. Eliot's poetry from a book he wrote called *Old Possum's Book of Practical Cats.*"

"Poems?" Erin said.

Zoe had to smile at the look on Erin's face. "I'm sure you'll like the show. And the dancing is spectacular."

"It was wonderful of you to get tickets for us, Zoe," Kathy said. She didn't really think her friends were showing enough appreciation.

"Yes, thanks," Jill and Lia chimed.

"Well, thank Kathy's father. He's the one who paid for them. Now, what about tomorrow?"

"I want to go to the Met," Kathy said.

"The Met?" Jill asked quizzically.

"The Metropolitan Museum of Art. Remember, we talked about it this morning, and I told you I wanted to spend some time there."

The silence was deafening.

"Gee, we haven't been to Soho yet," Jill said timidly.

"And we haven't done hardly any shopping at all," Erin added. "Looking, maybe, but not shopping."

Zoe tried to smooth things over. "Oh, you'll love the museum," she told the girls. "Besides the art, there's the wonderful fashion collection that Kathy wants to see."

Lia wanted to diffuse the tension too. "Costumes?" she asked, and when Zoe nodded, Lia said, "That sounds great."

"Maybe you won't be able to make it," Kathy said. "After all, you have to meet your cousin."

Kathy looked decidedly unhappy that Lia was having to take time away to visit with relatives. Didn't Kathy realize she wasn't all that happy about it either?

"We can go first thing in the morning," Zoe said. "That will give us some time before Lia has to leave for lunch."

Kathy stuck out her chin. "So then it's settled. We're going to the museum."

"It's your birthday," Jill said.

Thanks for remembering, Kathy thought bitterly.

Six

Lia opened her eyes, and it took a few seconds for her to remember exactly where she was. Then it all became clear. Zoe hadn't wanted her to share the guest room with Maddy, because she was afraid Lia might catch Maddy's bug, so she'd asked Lia to sleep out on the living-room couch.

It hadn't been too bad. The couch was one of those deep leather ones, so sleeping on it was sort of like sinking into a water bed. Maybe it was the odd sleeping arrangement that had encouraged all the strange dreams she'd had. Lia sat up a little. Now they were all coming back to her. And the dreams hadn't just been odd; parts of them had been wonderful.

Everything was all mixed up in them: the girls were squabbling; Cousin Sylvia was serving tea; and up in the air were gigantic clown balloons like the ones in the Macy's Thanksgiving Day parade. Then one of the clowns had come alive and was about to corner Lia and her friends. Just then, Hank had appeared and punctured the clown with a giant hat pin. Then he scooped Lia up in his arms and took her out of harm's way. Lia had noted with satisfaction that he left the other girls to shift for themselves.

But that wasn't the end of the dream. Hank had carried Lia around the corner, and he'd looked into her eyes in the dreamiest way. Then Lia had woken up. She closed her eyes and snuggled under the cover, trying to recover the way she'd felt when he looked at her. It was delicious.

She wouldn't have minded just reliving that moment for the next hour or two, but then she remembered that Zoe had said Hank was going to bring over bagels for breakfast. Popping up like a jack-in-the-box, Lia hurried off the couch. She didn't want to be in her striped flannel pajamas when he showed up.

Maddy was still asleep, but she opened her eyes when Lia walked softly into the room.

"How are you?" Lia asked with concern.

Maddy furrowed her brow as if she was trying to decide. "Not as bad as yesterday. But not great."

Lia touched Maddy's head, even though she wasn't quite sure what she was feeling for. "I don't think you're hot."

"Mmm." Maddy snuggled back under the covers. "I guess I'll go back to sleep for a while."

"Good idea." Lia grabbed some clothes and tiptoed out to the bathroom.

Lia had called Sylvia back last night, and they had set up a luncheon date at one of the restaurants near the museum. She didn't think there would be time to change afterward, so she put on the dressy outfit her mother had insisted she bring to wear to *Cats*.

Even though she usually wore jeans and sweaters or sweatshirts, Lia had to admit she liked the soft red sweater and the short plaid skirt that she wore over red tights. She brushed her blond hair and then tied it back with a ribbon.

When Lia stepped out of the bathroom, she expected everyone else to be awake, but it was still quiet. Feeling as if she should tiptoe, Lia walked into the kitchen, looked at the old-fashioned round kitchen clock, and then did a double take. She had glanced at the little alarm clock when she'd checked on Maddy, and she thought it had said eight-thirty. But she must have read the clock in the bedroom wrong, because it was only ten after eight now.

"This must be what people mean when they say 'all dressed up with nowhere to go,'" Lia murmured as she poured herself some orange juice. She felt a little foolish, but she figured it wouldn't be long before she was joined by her friends. On the other hand, at least it was peaceful now. No telling it what it would be like when they were all together again.

Lia took her juice to the kitchen table and sat down. What was the problem? she wondered. Everyone had been so excited about coming to New York. Sure, they were tired when they arrived, but they had had plenty of time to rest between sight-seeing jaunts. No, it just seemed as if everyone was out of sorts, with Kathy the grumpiest of all.

Lia was startled to hear a key turn in the lock. For a moment she was frightened. Then she remembered that Hank was expected. Sure enough, he came in carrying two brown bags full of food.

Immediately, Lia flashed back to her dream and felt embarrassed. "Hi," she mumbled, barely looking up, as Hank set the bags down on the table.

"Wow, you look lovely," Hank said.

"Thank you," Lia squeaked. "I'm having lunch with my dad's cousin."

"Well, you'll be the hit of the room," Hank said as he put away the orange juice.

He flashed her a smile, and Lia thought she might die.

"Where is everyone?" Hank asked.

"Still sleeping, I guess."

"Zoe loves to sleep in on Saturday. I guess your friends do too."

"Uh-huh." Can't you say something more interesting? Lia scolded herself. She sounded like she was five.

"I wanted to get here early and have breakfast on the table, but traffic was so bad this morning, I figured you'd all be up."

"Not yet."

"How about I toast us a couple of bagels while we wait," Hank said. "Are you hungry?"

"Absolutely." There. She had used a word with more than two syllables.

"So how's the trip been so far?"

Lia was ready to say what she was sure Hank expected to hear. The trip was great, everyone was having a wonderful time, blah, blah. But he was being so nice. Maybe he could help.

"Well, Zoe is showing us a wonderful time," Lia began. She didn't want him to think any of this was his girlfriend's fault.

Hank looked up from slicing the bagels. "But . . ."

"I don't know," Lia said helplessly. "We're just not getting along the way we usually do."

"Have you talked about it?"

"Not really. Either we're too tired or too busy. It's just not going well. I hope—"

Before she could continue, Kathy appeared in the doorway. "What's not going well?"

Startled, Lia said, "Nothing. I mean, I was . . ."

"Good morning, Kathy," Hank said, smiling at Kathy. "How about some breakfast?"

Kathy looked at the bagels on the table. "I guess. But what were you talking about?"

"Oh, Lia was just telling me about a paper she's doing in school," Hank said to Lia's relief.

Kathy looked like she wasn't sure she believed Hank, but before she could say anything else, he asked, "Poppy seed? Raisin? Onion?"

"Not onion," Kathy said, wrinkling her nose. "Raisin, I guess."

"Fine. With cinnamon cream cheese then. That's a winning combination. Let me fix it for you."

"Okay." Kathy brightened a little.

Boy, Lia thought. *Just like my dream. Hank swoops down and saves me. Of course, that means Kathy is the evil clown balloon.* A small giggle escaped her lips.

"What's so funny?" Kathy asked.

"Nothing. I'm just enjoying myself."

"Well, that's good," Kathy said, mollified. She turned to go to the refrigerator, and Lia and Hank exchanged a smile.

The others straggled out of bed, and it took a while for them all to get ready, but eventually everyone except Maddy was set to go to the museum. Zoe wanted to forestall a relapse, so she insisted Maddy take it easy today.

Even though she was disappointed, Maddy had to agree staying in was probably a wise choice. She was sitting up in bed by this time, and had gotten her breakfast served on a tray, so at least she was feeling pampered. Everyone came in to visit, and Zoe gave her some magazines and the remote control for the television, so she wouldn't get bored.

"I'm going to take a pass on the museum," Hank said, as he drained his second cup of coffee.

"Don't you like museums?" Erin asked innocently enough, but Kathy gave her a look anyway.

"No, I love them, especially the Metropolitan, but I visit there fairly often, and I have to go into the office today. So have a good time. If I have a chance, I'll stop by before you go to the theater."

It was a cold crisp day, so everyone decided to walk through the park to the museum.

"Does it snow here much?" Lia asked Zoe.

"Oh sure, but not like in Chicago. Most of the time it's pretty easy to get around."

"I just can't get over all the people," Jill said, shaking her head. "Where do they all come from?"

"Everywhere," Zoe said, laughing, and it was true. Every color and nationality seemed to be represented on the streets of New York.

"The hike up those steps looks pretty long," Jill noted when they arrived at the stately Metropolitan Museum with its grand staircase leading up to the door.

"Hey, that should be no problem for a skater like you," Kathy said. "Your legs are made of iron, aren't they?"

"They used to be when I was skating regularly. Now I think they're made of pudding."

Although the girls hadn't expected to be impressed by the museum, it was hard not to. It was a spectacular building with dauntingly high ceilings, and of course impressive paintings and statues everywhere. Nevertheless, a little of the museum went a long way.

"How many pictures do you think there are in here?" Erin asked Jill.

"Lots," Jill replied glumly.

Kathy, who had been enjoying almost all the artwork, noticed how the others were dragging around. "Well, I guess we should get over to the fashion collection," she said a bit disgustedly, "or you guys are going to fall over before we see one dress."

Lia, trying to make peace, said, "Yes, I don't have much time before I have to go meet my relatives."

"I think it was just a little rude setting up this date with your cousin when we were supposed to spend the day at the museum," Kathy said, taking out some of her disappointment at the lack of enthusiasm on Lia.

Lia looked at her with surprise. "What do you mean? I've said all along that I was going have to set aside time to see family. My parents would kill me if I didn't."

"I know, I know," Kathy muttered. "It just seems like everything's interfering with my plans."

"Well, maybe my lunch date will be the last interference," Lia replied, with a little sarcastic inflection.

But Lia was wrong. The group had barely gotten to the fashion collection, where they were looking at some Hollywood costumes, when Zoe sat down heavily on one of the stone benches. She gave a small *oomph* sound that made the others turn around.

"What's wrong?" Kathy asked, a little alarmed. Zoe looked like if she hadn't sat down, she might have fallen down.

"I don't feel well. It just hit me."

"I wonder if you have the same thing Maddy does," Lia said worriedly.

"I wouldn't be surprised," Zoe said.

Great, Kathy thought, *just great.* It wasn't bad enough that Maddy was sick, she had spread her germs to Zoe as well. Kathy wondered if they were going to start dropping like flies. Then she felt guilty for thinking of herself when Zoe obviously wasn't feeling well at all.

"I think we're going to have to cut this short," Zoe said. "I'm sorry, Kathy. I know how much you wanted to come here."

"Oh, that's okay," Kathy said, giving her a hug. "I just want you to feel better." And at that moment, she meant it, too.

With Zoe leaning on Kathy, they quickly managed to grab a cab and head back to the apartment.

"I don't know what to do about this afternoon," Zoe fretted. "It's such a great day. I hate to have you just sit around the apartment."

Erin knew it wasn't very nice of her, but ever since Zoe had sat down, Erin couldn't help thinking that this was an incredible break. She had pretty much decided that there was no way she was going to be able to meet Kevin. And perhaps a little part of her thought that was probably a good thing.

But now it seemed that fate had intervened. Zoe was definitely going to bed, and it would be much easier to slip away from the rest of the girls.

"Uh, Zoe, I need to do an errand this afternoon," Erin said.

"Errand?" Zoe said weakly.

"It's really just in the neighborhood. I have to buy something."

It was true. She hadn't gotten Kathy a present yet. So she and Kevin could buy something along the way.

"Oh," Zoe said, catching her meaning, even through her fog. "That would be all right, I guess."

Out of the corner of her eye, Erin could feel Jill sending a look her way, but she ignored it. "Thanks."

"Just don't be wandering around on your own," Zoe said, leaning back against the cab seat and closing her eyes.

"No, I won't," Erin replied. Then for the rest of the ride Erin thought about Kevin holding her hand, showing her all the sights of New York.

SEVEN

Getting away was not as easy as Erin had thought it would be. She'd supposed she would slip out in the middle of the confusion. And as she'd expected, there was plenty. Once they arrived at the apartment, they all helped Zoe get to bed. Kathy found her a pair of clean pajamas, Erin located the aspirin in the medicine cabinet, and Jill fixed her a cup of tea. Lia headed for the phone and was relieved to catch Sylvia before she left the house. They changed their plans to meet at a restaurant just down the street from Zoe's apartment. Then Kathy called Hank to let him know about Zoe. She relayed Zoe's message asking if he'd use her ticket this evening for *Cats*.

But even with everything that was going on, there was still no chance for Erin to make an early getaway. Maddy, who was up and about and feeling much better, cornered Erin and began a discussion, wanting to know how Zoe got sick, and if Erin thought that perhaps Maddy had given Zoe her germs. So Erin had to spend a good fifteen minutes giving her all the details and reassuring her that the sudden onset of the flu wasn't her fault. And perhaps it wasn't, because Zoe was feeling queasy in her stomach, which had not been one of Maddy's symptoms.

Finally, Erin had a moment to try and spruce herself up, but when she ducked into her bedroom, Jill was right behind her.

"So you're going," Jill said. It wasn't a question.

"I thought I might."

"Might, yeah right. Don't lie to me. You're heading over to that Tower Records, and it isn't to buy Kathy a birthday present."

"I might," Erin said defensively.

"Like I said. Well, if you remember, I don't have a present for Kathy either, so I guess you won't mind me walking over to Tower Records with you."

"What!"

"Don't raise your eyebrows or your voice like that to me. Do you really think I'm going to let you go off on this adventure all by your lonesome?"

"I don't know why not," Erin said huffily. "I'd let you go by yourself."

"I wouldn't do anything this dumb. I swear I'd tell Zoe, only I don't want to make her sicker."

"Come on," Erin said, a little pleadingly. "It's an adventure. Besides Kevin's not a weirdo or anything. You met him."

"Yeah, for two minutes. You've known him about five minutes longer than that."

"He was in the Macy's Thanksgiving Day parade, Jill."

"Oh well, in that case, let's nominate him for president."

"Very funny," Erin said. Now she was starting to get mad. "Is there any special reason why you have to throw a big bucket of cold water on my good time?"

Erin's temper was kicking in. Jill knew from experience that you couldn't talk to Erin at all when she was mad. "Hey," Jill said, trying not to sound so hostile. "I'm sorry you're looking at it that way. I just don't want you to do anything ... unsafe." She almost said stupid.

Erin calmed down too. "I know you want to look out for me, Jill, but . . ."

"Then you won't mind if I just walk with you down to Tower Records. You could get lost, and then you'd never find that boy of yours."

Erin could see she wasn't going anywhere without Jill. "All right, but just to the record store. Then we split up."

We'll see, Jill thought. "I'll be ready in fifteen minutes."

"I'll be ready in ten." But it took Erin a little longer than that. First she had to find just the right thing to wear, and that wasn't easy with the meager amount of clothing she had brought with her. The dress she was wearing to the theater tonight was way too fancy, and the flannel shirt she had worn yesterday and this morning was way past its prime. Then she remembered the blue striped sweater that Lia had brought with her. It would be perfect, and Erin was sure that Lia wouldn't mind if she wore it. Of course, she couldn't ask her, because she had already left for lunch. But Erin was already convinced that it wouldn't be a problem. She hurried off to Lia's bedroom to try it on.

"Hey," Maddy said, coming into the bedroom she shared with Lia. "Isn't that Lia's sweater?"

Erin looked down at herself as if she were surprised to find herself wearing it. "Oh, yeah. I sort of ran out of clothes."

"Are you going somewhere special?"

Erin didn't want to lie to Maddy, but she knew if she mentioned Kevin it would lead to a lot more questions. "Jill and I are going to Tower Records to get Kathy a present." That part was at least true.

"Oh, maybe I'll come with you."

This was turning into a parade about as long as the one they'd seen on Thursday, Erin thought. "Weren't you going to stay in until it was time to go to the theater?"

"That was the plan," Maddy said, "but I'm going stir-crazy in here."

"You feel well enough to walk to Tower? It's about ten blocks away."

"Ten blocks," Maddy said doubtfully.

Erin shrugged.

"Maybe that *is* a little far."

"You want to be well enough to see *Cats*," Erin said. She felt a little bad about trying to get Maddy to stay home, but on the other hand, everything she was saying was true.

"All right," Maddy said with a sigh. "If I give you some money will you buy Kathy a CD for me?"

"Sure," Erin said. "Lia told me a bunch that Kathy wanted."

Erin went to get Jill and picked up the money from Maddy, and they were just about to walk out the door when Kathy appeared in the hallway. "So you're going out," she said sourly.

"Well, you wouldn't want to come with us, Kathy," Erin said. "It might ruin a surprise."

"I certainly wouldn't want anything else ruined."

Jill looked at Kathy sympathetically. "I know you feel bad that Zoe got sick, but it's not going to change any of our plans. We're still going to *Cats* and everything."

"Yeah, I guess."

Erin and Jill exchanged glances.

"How are you going to spend this afternoon?" Jill asked.

"Maddy's learning how to play chess, and Zoe has a board, so I'm going to have a lesson. But you two won't be gone very long, will you?"

Jill didn't say anything, so it was left for Erin to say, "Not very."

"Maybe we can at least take a walk when you get back." Kathy didn't sound angry anymore, just plaintive.

As soon as the door closed behind them, Jill said, "Did you hear that? All Kathy wants out of this afternoon is a crummy walk, and you won't even be here to do that."

Now Erin was feeling even worse than she had when she was talking to Maddy. Clearly, Kathy was unhappy about the way things were going, and Erin hadn't done much to make them better. "Maybe I should just come back with you."

"Now you're thinking," Jill said approvingly.

But when they arrived at the record store, a mammoth place teeming with people, Erin almost immediately saw Kevin over in the rock section. He looked so tall and terrific that all thought of going back to Zoe's went completely out of Erin's head.

"There he is!" Erin said, clutching her friend's arm.

"I was hoping you wouldn't find him in this mob," Jill said, but she sounded resigned.

Erin walked over to him, trying to be cool. She tapped him on the shoulder. "Hi."

"You made it," Kevin said. "Can you believe it? This place is huge."

"Haven't you ever been here before?" Jill asked curiously. Kevin seemed as impressed with the store as they were.

"Ah, not really," Kevin said vaguely. "I never got around to it."

Jill thought that was a little odd for a native New Yorker, but Erin didn't seem to notice.

"So, are you going to show me the sights?" Erin asked.

"Sure." He glanced over at Jill, and the look was not especially welcoming. "Are you both going?"

Before Jill could answer, Erin said. "No. Jill just walked me over."

Jill shot Erin a dirty look. Now if she said she was going, she'd look like an idiot. "You don't have much time," Jill said. At least she would remind Erin of that. Turning to Kevin, she said, "We're going to have a birthday dinner for Kathy, and we've got to make the curtain for *Cats*."

"*Cats?*" Kevin asked.

"It's a musical. You never heard of it?"

"Yeah, sure. It's about cats, right?"

Jill snickered. "Right."

Kevin looked offended. "Well, if you all have so much stuff happening, then Erin and I better get going."

Erin's expression was pleading. "Jill, tell the others I just wanted to do a little more shopping."

"Oh sure," Jill snapped. "No problem." Without saying good-bye, she walked away.

"What's with her?"

Erin watched Jill's receding figure. "She doesn't think I should be going all over New York with a strange boy."

"I'm not strange," Kevin said with a smile. "Well, not too strange, anyway." He put his hand lightly on Erin's shoulder. She didn't know if she should be thrilled, or worried that Kevin might be moving a little too fast. She decided to be thrilled.

"So what are you going to show me?" Erin asked.

"I thought maybe we could go to a movie. There's that new Schwarzenegger flick down the street."

"A movie?" Erin repeated with surprise. "I thought we were going to do some more sight-seeing."

"Didn't you do that yesterday?"

"Well, just a little. But there's a lot more I want to see."

Kevin shrugged. "Whatever."

They headed outside. The temperature had taken a nosedive, and a wind had started up.

"Let's walk for a while," Kevin said.

"It's getting pretty cold," Erin said doubtfully. "Maybe we should just take the subway somewhere. Like Chinatown or SoHo. I haven't been there yet."

"SoHo?"

"Yeah, you know, it's supposed to be really neat. Or Chinatown, we could have lunch. I'm really getting hungry."

"Okay, well, let's start walking anyway."

Erin jammed her hands in her pockets. After a few blocks, she took off her muffler and put it around her head.

Kevin looked at her and started to laugh.

"What's so funny?" Erin asked crossly.

"You look like somebody's grandmother."

"Sorry. I left my hat at home."

There wasn't much conversation as they walked along. Kevin seemed a little put out about something, but she couldn't figure out what she had done. Erin tried to get Kevin to tell her about *Star Trek,* but he didn't have much to say on that topic either.

"It's just a TV show."

"But they shoot it in Los Angeles, don't they? Were you living out there?"

"No."

"Oh," Erin said, puzzled. "So you were visiting?"

"Yeah. I was visiting. My uncle, he does publicity for the show, and that's how I got on."

They wandered down past an open plaza surrounded by white stone buildings. "We were here yesterday," Erin said. "What's this place called again?"

Kevin looked at a sign. "Lincoln Center."

"That's right. Where they have plays and the opera."

Erin waited for Kevin to make a comment, but none was forthcoming.

"Do you ever try out for plays?"

Kevin looked at her with surprise. "Why would I do that?"

"Because you're an actor," Erin said with exasperation.

"Oh, I'm not exactly an actor."

"So that *Star Trek* show was just a one-time thing?"

"Uh-huh."

"What other kinds of things do you do in your spare time?"

Kevin shrugged. "I play ball. Basketball."

Talking to this guy was harder than pulling teeth. Erin was tempted to just turn around and go home— she was pretty sure she could find her way back—but she did want to have lunch in Chinatown. "Why don't we get on a subway and go to Chinatown? I'm starving, aren't you?"

Kevin just shrugged again. "I could eat, I guess. But I don't see why we don't just grab something here. There's a million restaurants around."

Erin looked at Kevin curiously. "Don't you know how to get to Chinatown?"

Indignantly, Kevin responded, "Of course I do. You want to go to Chinatown, we'll go to Chinatown."

"Great," Erin said, perking up a little. Finally, things were working out. Maybe this afternoon wouldn't be such a waste after all.

EIGHT

"I'm really starting to worry," Maddy whispered to Lia. She didn't want Zoe, who was weakly sitting up in the bedroom across the hall, to hear her. Although Zoe seemed to be feeling a little better, she had slept most of the afternoon and had no idea that Erin was missing.

"I've been worried since I got back from lunch." Lia's lunch with her cousin Sylvia had gone better than Lia had expected. She had only the vaguest of memories of her father's cousin, so she hadn't known what to expect. She thought that Sylvia would be like so many adults, on the boring side. Lia, who tended to be shy, wondered if they would even be able to keep a conversation going.

But from the moment Lia had walked into the nearby restaurant and seen Sylvia waving her over, she had realized that Sylvia wasn't going to be dull.

Sylvia was about the age of Lia's own parents, in her late thirties, but she could have passed for half that age. She was tall, with blond hair cascading down her back, and she had the kind of figure that Lia knew would never be hers. She wore tight leather pants and a pink angora sweater, an outfit Lia had seen in magazines but never in real life. When Sylvia waved her over to their table, the heads of all the men in the place turned to see who was lucky enough to be Sylvia's dining companion. Lia was not what they expected.

The restaurant Sylvia had chosen for lunch seemed surprisingly sedate for a woman who looked like a rock star. The oak-paneled room was hushed and the china on the table was fine and fragile. Lia was a little worried that she might make too much noise, or worse, knock over one of those delicate plates, but Sylvia didn't seem to have the same concerns. She called the waiter over with a sweep of her hand.

When lunch was finally ordered Sylvia leaned back in her chair and said, "You look almost nothing like your father."

"No, I look like my mom."

"Pretty hair like hers," Sylvia agreed.

Lia considered this quite a compliment from a woman who had such beautiful blond hair herself.

"I'm sorry you didn't get to meet my daughters, but I decided they might be a little young for a formal lunch. Maybe it's better this way; we can just talk. So tell me, how's the trip? I want to hear about everything you've done."

Maybe it was because Sylvia, as she told Lia to call her, seemed so interested. Or perhaps it was just waiting to spill out anyway, but Lia told her the whole story of the trip, all the disasters and disappointments, and how Kathy especially seemed to be getting more and more in a funk.

"Well, you can't blame her," Sylvia said, enjoying the crab salad that was now in front of her. "It's probably not turning out at all as she expected."

"I guess that's it."

"Of course, sometimes hostesses expect too much from their guests, but in this case, I think Kathy does have reason to be disappointed. There's nothing much fun about sickness and sugary sweet potatoes."

"So what should I do?" Lia asked. Sylvia seemed so

self assured. Lia had a lot of confidence she'd come up with the right answer.

"First of all, eat your hamburger. Starving yourself isn't going to help anything. And while you're doing that, I'll think."

They ate in companionable silence for a few minutes. Then Sylvia said, "Is there something special you could do? Something that would really please Kathy? Something that would show how much you want this weekend to be special for her?"

Lia thought about it. "Kathy's family has loads of money. Anything we could buy her, she could get for herself."

"No, no, not a gift from a store. A gift of love."

At first nothing came to mind. Then it hit Lia, the one thing that Kathy really wanted. "She would really like to hear from Rick."

Sylvia raised an eyebrow. "And he is . . . ?"

"Her boyfriend from camp. He lives in Boston, and the last time they talked, it didn't go very well."

"Do you have his phone number?"

Lia shook her head. Then she remembered something. "Rick's a Junior, so his dad's name is Derek Weller, too."

"Well, then you can try directory assistance in Boston."

Lia could hardly wait to finish lunch. If she could actually get in touch with Rick, it might turn Kathy's whole birthday weekend around.

As they were walking out of the restaurant, Sylvia spotted the phone booth. It was the old-fashioned kind with a door that closed. "Lots of privacy in there," Sylvia pointed out.

Suddenly, Lia got nervous.

Sylvia took a pen and paper out of her purse and scribbled down a number. "This is directory assistance in Boston. Do you need money? I've got lots of change."

"No. My folks gave me their phone card so I could call them. I suppose I could make a call to Boston on it."

"Your folks won't mind if you explain it was for a good cause."

Lia wasn't so sure about that, but she could always pay them back when the bill arrived. Rather reluctantly, Lia went into the booth and called directory assistance. Rick's number was listed, so, taking a deep breath, Lia dialed his house. She could feel her heart pounding as the phone rang. What was she going to say, exactly? Wouldn't she seem like a big buttinsky? The phone rang for the fourth time. *Maybe no one's home,* Lia thought, with more relief than regret, but just then Rick answered. Once they started talking, the awkwardness quickly melted away. Lia explained where she and the other girls were and why.

"So that's where she is," Rick said.

"You were trying to reach her?"

"I knew it was Kathy's birthday. I called her at her mom's, but no one was home. I was getting up my courage to call her father's house."

"Then you aren't mad anymore?" Lia asked.

"I was never that mad."

"Then why didn't you . . ."

"Why didn't I call?"

"Yeah. Or write."

"I don't know. It's been so tough getting into living in Boston. My school's much harder here than the one at home. I just didn't feel like talking to anyone, I guess. I can get in some pretty bad funks."

"I remember," Lia told him.

"I was just being stupid like I was at camp. I really miss Kathy."

"That's good," Lia said encouragingly. "So if I give you the number at Zoe's, you'll call tomorrow?"

"Sure. I would have felt terrible if I missed her birthday." More softly, he added, "Thanks for calling."

Lia was very pleased with herself when Sylvia dropped her off at Zoe's. She could hardly wait to let the others know about the surprise she had arranged for Kathy.

But the surprise was on her. When she walked in, she was hit with the news that Erin was touring the town with some kid off a *Star Trek* float and hadn't been heard from since early in the afternoon.

When she came back from the record store, Jill's immediate thought had been not to mention anything to anyone. She would just cross her fingers and hope that Erin would turn up sooner or later. But Maddy had wanted to know where Erin was, and Jill, tired of keeping the secret to herself, had told her.

Now Lia arrived home to hear the whole miserable story. Only Kathy, who had gone out with Hank to pick up her birthday cake, wasn't caught up.

By five o'clock, the girls were beginning to wonder if Kathy had disappeared as well. "She should have been home hours ago," Maddy groaned. "How long could it take to pick up a cake?"

"Maybe we should tell Zoe," Lia said worriedly.

"About Kathy? Or Erin, too?" Jill asked. "This is turning into a nightmare."

"Why don't we start with Kathy," Lia said. "Hank might have told Zoe he had to make another stop."

The girls decided they would seem less concerned if they came into Zoe's room with some tea and toast. That way they could look like angels of mercy, not the bearers of bad news.

When the tray was all fixed up, Lia, with the others behind her, carried it to Zoe's room.

"Knock, knock," she said to Zoe, who was listlessly leafing through a magazine.

"How sweet," Zoe said, sitting up a little. "I didn't think I had any appetite, but maybe I could try some toast and tea." She looked at the three of them. "Isn't Kathy back yet?"

"Not yet," Jill said carefully.

"Wasn't it nice of Hank to take her back to the Metropolitan? I'm sure she felt terrible about missing the fashion collection."

The girls exchanged a glance of relief.

Zoe looked at them as she swallowed a sip of the tea. "Oh, gosh, maybe you didn't know. Hank said they could spend an hour or so there. They're going to get Chinese food, too. You must have wondered what happened to them."

"We did," Maddy said.

"I'm sorry, I'm so out of it, I guess I thought you knew. They should be home soon with dinner, and then you'll have to hustle over to the theater to make the eight o'clock curtain." She turned to Maddy. "How are you feeling now?"

"Much better."

Zoe took another sip of the tea, then put it back on the tray with its untouched toast. "This is about all I can manage right now. Thanks for bringing it, though."

Jill grabbed the tray, and the girls were about to leave when Zoe said, "Where's Erin?"

Before any of them could think of an answer, the door in the front hall slammed.

"That must be Kathy," Lia said.

Or maybe it's Erin, they all thought to themselves. In any event, it was a good reason to leave Zoe, her question still hanging in the air.

"Oh, it's you," Lia said when they got into the hall and saw Kathy and Hank hanging up their coats.

"That's not a very nice greeting," Hank said reprovingly, and Lia felt wounded.

Kathy practically slammed the closet door. "I'm getting used to it. Boy, a more ungrateful group of friends . . ."

"What do you mean?" Jill asked.

"Oh, never mind," Kathy said grumpily. "Let's just decide how we're going to organize this night. Eat first or dress first?"

"Eat first," Maddy said.

"I agree," Jill seconded. "I don't want to spill anything on anything."

"So fine, we'll eat." Kathy took the two shopping bags of Chinese food into the kitchen.

As soon as she was out of earshot, Lia said, "Aren't we getting a little ahead of ourselves? We may not be going anywhere."

"What do you mean?" Hank asked with a frown.

Lia looked at her friends, and then plunged in. "It's Erin. She's not here."

"What?"

"Jill, you tell him."

Kathy reappeared. "Tell him what?"

Hank said, "I think we better go into the living room

and sit down. This isn't something we want Zoe to hear, is it?" he asked with a sigh.

Lia and Jill shook their heads. Then they all went into the living room, and Jill told him the story of Kevin O'Rourke, Star Trekker and tour guide.

Hank was visibly shaken by Jill's story. "You mean, Erin is missing?"

"I guess so," Lia said quietly.

"I tried to stop her," Jill said, very upset. "She just wouldn't listen."

"I can't believe she did this," Kathy said, seething.

"Aren't you worried about her?" Lia asked.

"No. I'm sure she's out having a great time. And the heck with everyone else."

Hank turned to Jill. "How did this kid look?"

Jill shrugged. "He was a pretty tall, brown hair . . ."

"I mean did he look normal?"

"Yeah. He didn't look like a weirdo or anything."

"How old was he?"

"About our age."

"Well, that's something," Hank muttered. "Now what?"

"You could call the police," Maddy suggested.

"She's only been missing a couple of hours. And I don't think the police would even consider this missing. They'd probably just tell me to call later if she hasn't shown up."

Kathy got up. "Well, I know what I'm going to do."

"What?" Jill asked.

"Eat dinner and then go see *Cats.*"

"You can eat?" Lia didn't think she could swallow a bite.

"I'm not going to have another meal ruined. Now does anyone else want to have dinner with me?"

The girls looked at Hank.

"I guess we should try to eat something," Hank said. "Everything's worse on an empty stomach."

So the girls set the table, and Hank and Kathy brought out the food in its white cartons. The conversation at dinner was minimal, with lots of "Please pass the egg rolls," or "Can I have the moo shu," although none of them, even Kathy, ate very much at all. No one felt like cake, and no one mentioned it.

Hank cleared while the girls got dressed.

"How are you feeling?" Lia asked Maddy. Lia wasn't changing clothes, so she sat on the bed and watched Maddy get ready.

"My fever's gone. I still feel a little weak. Lia, are we doing the right thing by going to the play? Should we wait here to find out about Erin?"

The others must have been thinking the same thing, because it was a very reluctant group that waited in the hallway for Kathy to join them. When she did come out of her room, she looked beautiful. Her hair was pulled back and she was wearing a beige cashmere turtleneck and a pair of dressy wool trousers. She could easily have passed for sixteen.

"You look great," Maddy said sincerely.

Kathy gave her a smile that was the first genuine one in a while. Then she looked at her watch. "We should get going."

Lia cleared her throat. "Maybe one of us should stay. What if Erin comes home, and she's upset?"

"*She's* upset?" Kathy said, her voice rising.

Hank came in from the kitchen. "I don't know what to do about tonight. I thought maybe I should stick around here and see if she shows up, but I don't want you to go down to the theater district—or try to get home—by yourselves. But if I don't stay, we'll have to tell Zoe."

Lia felt sorry for Hank. He looked totally out of his element.

No one seemed to know what to do. The girls were upset, and going off to a play was the last thing that any of them, except perhaps Kathy, wanted to do.

The thick silence was interrupted by the shrill ring of the telephone. As Hank picked it up, each of the girls willed it to be Erin. Hank nodded to them as he heard Erin's hello.

"Erin, where are you?"

"At the Winter Garden Theatre. Where *Cats* is playing."

"And where have you been?"

"Queens."

"Queens?"

"Lost in Queens."

NINE

Erin was in big trouble, and she knew it. Hank had sounded mad when he said, "I don't want you to move. Just wait in front of the theater. We're already running late. And when we get there," he added ominously, "you've got a lot of talking to do."

As she watched the well-dressed theatergoers streaming into the Winter Garden, Erin wondered how she was going to get out of this mess. Maybe she could pretend she was getting sick like Maddy and Zoe. Would everyone still be mad at her if they thought she was ill? Yeah, they probably would. And she couldn't say she didn't deserve it. She had been an idiot. And only now, standing safely in front of the theater, did she realize how lucky she was to be only embarrassed. With her running around in strange neighborhoods with a boy she barely knew, things could have been so much worse.

Erin hoped that it would take the others forever to arrive at the theater. Twenty minutes later, they came walking around the corner. None of them looked happy.

As soon as she was within earshot, Hank demanded, "Erin, let's hear the whole story."

"I'll tell you, but first, I've got to say something." Erin looked at the others, her face full of genuine misery. "I'm sorry. I mean, really sorry. Jill tried to tell me not to go, but I thought seeing New York with Kevin would be exciting. It was the worst."

"You're all right, though, aren't you?" Lia asked anxiously.

"Oh, sure. He wasn't creepy or anything. Just dumb. And a liar."

"A liar?" Jill repeated.

"He wasn't from New York City at all," Erin said disgustedly. "He was from Schenectady."

"Where's that?" Maddy wanted to know.

Hank supplied the answer. "Upstate New York. He told you he was from Manhattan?"

"Yes, he was going to show me the city. Well, I

wanted to go to Chinatown, and I should have guessed something was up from the way he kept trying to get me to stay around where we were. But finally, we got on the subway. He didn't even know how to use it."

"And that's how you ended up in Queens?" Maddy asked.

"We got on some train. Kevin told me it was one to Chinatown, and then he said we had to change. We rode for a while, and then, all of a sudden, he hustled me off and we followed a lot of people outside. It looked totally different from Manhattan, but some of the street names were the same. We were on Thirty-Fifth Street, and I thought . . ."

"You thought you were on Thirty-Fifth Street in Manhattan," Hank finished for her.

Erin nodded miserably. "We walked around and around, and we never could figure out where we were, even after Kevin pulled out a map. I finally figured out Kevin didn't know what he was doing."

"Didn't they have phones in Queens?" Kathy asked icily.

"I thought maybe I wouldn't have to phone. Kevin kept saying he'd get me right back, so I figured I'd still get home in plenty of time," Erin said glumly. "But

Kevin wouldn't ask anyone for directions. Finally, I asked and this lady told us where we were and how to get back and to change at Times Square for the Upper West Side. I knew the theater was near Times Square, so I decided that I was just going to get off and walk to *Cats,* but then Kevin and I had another fight . . ."

"Another fight?" Maddy asked, her eyes wide.

Hank sighed. "I'm afraid I don't have time for any more details. I've got to pick up the tickets at the window."

That was all right with Erin. She didn't feel like going into details, even though the girls were obviously ready to hear more. Actually, the fight had been one long one rather than several separate ones. It had started when they stepped off the subway and climbed the stairs to what was supposed to be Chinatown.

"Where are all the Chinese people?" Erin had asked, looking around.

Kevin shrugged. "Maybe they're inside."

"Inside where? There aren't even any Chinese restaurants around."

"So, maybe this isn't Chinatown," Kevin reluctantly replied.

"Then why did we get off the subway?"

"Lots of people were getting off," Kevin mumbled. "I figured this was it. You don't want to go too far on a train. Let's walk for a while. We'll find it."

"A while" turned into a long while. Finally, Erin looked at Kevin, eyes narrowed. "You don't know where we are, do you?"

"Jeez, so maybe I don't know exactly where we are. New York's a pretty big place, in case you haven't noticed."

"I noticed. But anyone who's lived in New York all his life should know where Chinatown is." Suddenly suspicious, Erin said, "You're not from New York at all, are you?"

"I am too."

"You are not."

"I'm from New York, the state of New York."

"What city?" Erin asked challengingly.

"Schenectady."

"I knew it! You don't know your way around here any better than I do. Now we're lost!"

"We're not lost."

Erin practically stamped her foot. "Then get me home."

That's where the fight had started, and though it

had ebbed and flowed, through all their wrong turns and false assumptions about where they were, it never really ended until Erin announced that she was getting off the train at Times Square.

"Well, then I'm going with you," Kevin had said grimly.

"Why? So I can get lost again?"

"So I can make sure you get where you need to be."

"That would be a first," Erin muttered.

At Times Square, Erin stalked off the train, and Kevin was right behind her. "I can find it myself," she said, turning and almost bumping right into him, but even finding a great big theater wasn't all that easy. It was nighttime and everything looked unfamiliar, and then Erin remembered Zoe saying that the Times Square area wasn't the best in town. There were hordes of people everywhere, and while some of them looked all dressed up, and on their way to dinner or a show, others looked downright unsavory.

Erin hurried over to a couple and asked where the Winter Garden was, with Kevin glaring right behind her.

"It's on Fifty-Third, isn't it?" the woman said, wrapping her red coat more tightly around her.

"No, it's across from that theater where they do the David Letterman show," her companion countered. "That's Fifty-Fifth."

"Why don't you just start walking uptown," the woman suggested to Erin. "You'll run into it eventually."

Those didn't seem like very good instructions to Erin, but she started walking anyway. She thought about calling Zoe's, but decided it would be better to wait until she had successfully made her way to the theater. Finally, she saw the word *Cats* in lights several blocks away and started running toward it.

Kevin didn't follow any farther. He just bitterly called after her, "Thanks for a great afternoon."

Erin stopped and said, "It could have been, if you'd just told the truth."

Kevin turned and stomped away, which made Erin so mad, she yelled after him, "I bet you were never on *Star Trek,* either."

He didn't bother to answer her parting shot.

Erin knew eventually she'd give her friends all the details, but she didn't want to do it here, in front of the theater waiting to go see *Cats.* "I'm really sorry," she repeated to all of them. "Can we talk about all this later?"

"That's so easy for you to say, isn't it?" Kathy said. She was furious with Erin, furious with all of them actually. However, since Erin was the one who had committed the most obvious transgression, it was easiest for Kathy to take out her pent-up emotions on her.

"Kathy, I know I screwed up . . ."

Kathy glanced at her watch. "Do you even know how many hours you were gone? Did you know we might have missed the show entirely if you hadn't called when you did? We weren't sure if we should go or wait around to see what happened to you."

"Well, Kathy was sure," Jill whispered to Lia. "She was going to go to the play no matter what."

Before Kathy or Erin could say anything else, Hank came over with the tickets and hustled them into the theater. They were among the last to go in.

Stepping over a few people, who didn't look pleased by their late arrival, the girls took their seats. There was no actual curtain to go up. The set, an alley with fire escapes and garbage cans, was already on the stage. As the lights lowered, cats, fantastically made up and wearing furry costumes of every stripe and shape began slinking out from the wings.

The thing about a musical, Jill thought as the cats performed intricate dance numbers and cavorted on the stage, *is that it's hard not to tap your feet while you watch. And when you're tapping your feet, it's hard to stay upset or mad.* Certainly, she was feeling more calm. So when the first act ended, Jill was confident that tempers would have cooled and the girls could start to get back to normal.

They filed out to the lobby, which was full of milling patrons.

"I'm going to call Zoe and see how she's feeling," Hank said. "Try to all be here when I get back."

"I guess that was for me." Erin sighed.

"Well, you did give us all a scare," Lia said.

"I know, I know, but I said I'm sorry about a million times."

"I don't think sorry is going to cut it this time," Kathy informed her.

Now Erin was starting to get mad. She had always been taught that if you faced up to your mistakes and apologized, that was the first step to making things right. Clearly though, Kathy wasn't having any of it.

"You don't have to take everything out on me," Erin told her.

"No, I guess there's plenty of blame to go around." Kathy's anger hadn't dissipated one whit during the first act. Truth be told, she had barely watched the show at all. "I wish I'd never even planned this stupid weekend." Then she walked back to her seat, alone.

Maddy whispered to Lia, "Did you know Kathy felt like that?"

"I knew that she was mad," Lia answered back, "but I didn't know how mad." Kathy's angry feelings were obviously beyond being improved by toe-tapping.

Though the second act of the play was perhaps even better than the first, none of the girls enjoyed it very much. Each was thinking in her own way that something was very wrong here. Like any friends, they had squabbles, even fights, but never had one of them actually seemed to dislike another. Kathy seemed sorry she'd ever met up with her Holiday Five friends.

Even the ride home was quiet. No one seemed to know what to say. Kathy looked moodily out the window. Erin was on the other side of the back seat, also staring out at the New York night scene whizzing by.

"So did you like it?" Hank finally asked.

All the girls murmured that they did.

Hank lapsed back into silence. He seemed very relieved when he finally got them upstairs and into the apartment. "I'm going to check on Zoe," he said, leaving the girls to themselves.

"So what do you want to do now?" Lia said as they hung up their coats.

"How about go to sleep?" Kathy suggested. "That's what I'm going to do."

"What about your birthday cake?" Lia asked. "We never even sang you 'Happy Birthday.'"

Kathy turned to her. "Don't you think it's a little late for that?"

"We really should talk, Kathy. Have one of those bull sessions like we used to have at camp."

"I don't think you'd want to hear what I have to say," Kathy said.

Hank came out of Zoe's room. "She's feeling a little better, but she's still got a lot of sleeping to do. Try not to disturb her." All the girls said that they'd take care of her, thanked Hank, and then drifted to their own rooms. Only Lia stayed while Hank got ready to go out again.

"You've been really nice to us," Lia said shyly. This might be the last time she was alone with Hank. She wanted to make sure that he knew all his efforts had been appreciated.

"I won't kid you. This is more than I bargained for."

"We're not always like this," Lia said earnestly.

"No?"

"Oh no." Then she realized Hank was teasing her. Hank smiled down at her. "You seem like a very nice girl, Lia."

The word *girl* stung. But of course, she realized, that's all she was to Hank. For a moment she felt silly. She hoped he hadn't recognized her crush. But then she didn't care. If anyone deserved to be the object of her crush, it was Hank. Handsome, helpful, and really, really nice. She knew she was going to remember Hank Chavis for a long time.

Hank interrupted her thoughts. "There seems to be a lot of tension among you girls."

"There is. I'm worried our friendship is falling apart," she fretted.

"Is there something you can do to patch all this up?" he asked.

"I'm going to try," Lia said. "But I'm not sure what to do."

"Even though everyone's angry now, you've got to remind them how great it is when you're all getting along."

"You're right," Lia said thoughtfully.

Hank patted her on the shoulder. "I'm counting on you."

As she shut the door behind him, Lia wondered if

she could change the situation. It was a long shot, but Hank's vote of confidence was a spur. She decided to give it one more shot before she went to bed.

Kathy came out of her room and stiffly asked, "Where are the sheets and things you used when you were sleeping on the couch? With Zoe sick, it's my turn tonight."

"Kathy, I still think we should all talk. It's not good for you to be so mad."

"But I am mad."

"Then let's talk."

"I don't want to," Kathy said. "I just want to go to bed. Where are the sheets?"

Silently, Lia showed Kathy where the linen closet was. Then she went to the guest room, where Maddy was already in her nightgown and climbing into bed.

"What's wrong?" Maddy asked. "I mean, besides everything."

Lia sighed and began undressing. "That's it, everything. I'm worried, Maddy."

"What about?"

"If we don't clear the air about this, it could be the end for the Holiday Five."

"Oh, we've had fights before," Maddy argued.

"But Kathy's really hurt. And now Erin's mad. And

Jill told me she's angry with Erin for putting her in the position of lying."

"I don't think Kathy's thrilled with me either," Maddy said.

"You couldn't help it if you were sick."

"No, but I knew I wasn't feeling well when I got on the plane. Kathy asked me this afternoon if I didn't know I was coming down with something when we left."

Buttoning her pajamas, Lia climbed into the bed next to Maddy. "We've only got until three o'clock tomorrow afternoon to make all this right, Maddy."

"Do you think we can do it?"

Lia sighed. "I haven't got a clue."

TEN

Lia woke up very early, so early the gray morning light was just beginning to filter through the blinds.

Lying in bed, she felt as though she was continuing a conversation she'd been having with herself before she fell asleep. The last thought in her mind before she'd drifted off was wondering how to make this weekend end up right. It was the first thought that eased into her brain before she even opened her eyes.

Going over the weekend, detail by detail, starting with staying over at Kathy's house Wednesday night, Lia tried to figure out where it had all gone wrong.

She remembered how the girls had grumbled about getting up so early Thursday morning. Jill had even groaned that if she had realized what four-thirty in the morning felt like, she would have passed up the trip entirely. Jill wasn't serious, but that comment couldn't have made Kathy feel very good. None of them had started off that cold morning with an air of happy expectation. They had acted like they were doing Kathy a favor by going to New York at all.

Then there was the matter of presents. Lia had the small silver necklace that she had picked out for Kathy's birthday, but she had only gone shopping for it at her mother's insistence. Like the others, Lia had just assumed that she'd be able to buy something more interesting in New York. But as it had turned out, things were too expensive, or they'd been too rushed, or Kathy had been around when someone wanted to make a purchase. Now the girls were basically presentless, and Kathy knew it.

If that wasn't enough, Kathy was sensitive to the way everyone had been distracted. Erin's mind had been on Kevin and devising ways to see him all weekend. Jill had been worried about that, too. Maddy had been sick, and Lia had to admit she had thought more about Hank, and even her cousin Sylvia, than she had about Kathy. Top that with the world's worst Thanksgiving dinner and Zoe getting sick, and no wonder Kathy was feeling like her birthday weekend had been jinxed. About the only ray of bright light was Rick's birthday call, and Kathy didn't know about that.

Maddy turned over and sat up. "Are you okay?" she asked. "You're just staring up at the ceiling."

"You're awake. How do you feel?"

Maddy thought about it. "Fine. I actually feel fine."

"That's good."

"I bet I know what you're thinking about," Maddy said. "The same thing we were talking about last night."

Lia nodded.

Maddy got out of bed and grabbed her robe. "Well, let's get going."

"Where are we going?" Lia asked, startled.

"You said yesterday we only have until three o'clock to make things better." She peered at the clock. "It's eight now. That gives us seven hours."

"To do what?" Lia asked. "We don't even have a plan."

"We don't really have time for one, do we? We're just going to have to wing it," Maddy said confidently.

"Who lit a fire under you?" Lia asked as she followed Maddy's example and got out of bed.

"I've been sick and missed most of this trip. Well, I'll

be darned if I'm going to miss the last day. And it's going to be a good one."

Lia looked at Maddy, amazed. Then she shrugged. If Maddy could get this whole mess sorted out, more power to her. The first thing Maddy did was tiptoe into Jill and Erin's room. Gently, Maddy woke them and said, "Get dressed, and be quiet about it. We're going to make a birthday party for Kathy."

Lia peeked into the living room where Kathy was buried under pillows and blankets. At camp, Kathy had a reputation for being able to sleep through thunderstorms, practical jokes, and the morning routine of four noisy cabinmates. This morning, her snoozability was going to be the key to getting a party on the table.

"I went in and told Zoe we were going out to buy some things," Jill whispered.

"Is she better?" Maddy wanted to know.

"A little, I think."

The girls tiptoed out the door and left it unlocked so they could get back in.

"It's so early," Jill said, as they rode down in the elevator. "Will anything be open?"

"This is New York," Maddy said. "Things stay open twenty-four hours."

But just in case, they asked the doorman where they would find a grocery store that would be open, and he directed them to one just a block away.

As they walked through the brisk morning air, the girls decided to clear their own air.

"Even if Kathy doesn't want to talk about what went wrong, I think we should," Lia said.

"It was my fault," Erin said glumly. "All of it."

"Not all of it, although your part was the most . . ." Lia fished around for a word, "dramatic."

"We've all been acting kind of stinky," Jill agreed.

"Kathy had a right to be mad at us," Maddy said. "Except for Lia, we don't even have a present for her."

"That's my fault, too," Erin said. "At least I could have picked up a CD at Tower Records."

"Well, it's too late for that now. Let's just hope we can get what we need for a party."

Luckily for the girls, though the store was the Mom-and-Pop type, it did have a little bit of everything. They were able to pick up festive paper plates and napkins that said *Happy Birthday,* fresh bagels and cream cheese, orange juice, and a lovely bouquet of flowers. They even found a corny birthday card covered with teddy bears. But there was nothing suitable as a gift.

"It's a start," Maddy said, as the woman behind the counter wrapped the flowers.

"We could buy some magazines for her," Erin said, looking around the store to find something that might work as a present.

"That seems a little cheap," Lia replied. "We'll just have to get her something when we get back home, I guess."

But as the girls were walking back to the apartment, they were startled to see the street outside Central Park coming alive with vendors setting up stands. Some of them had paintings that they were leaning against the wall of the park. One woman was putting up a card table with earrings and bracelets, while another was laying out velvety looking scarves.

"Are these for sale?" Maddy asked the scarf lady.

"I should hope so," the woman laughed.

"But what are you doing here?" Erin wanted to know.

"We're local artisans. We make these things," the woman replied. "We're always here on Sundays during the summer, and at Christmas time, if it's not too cold."

Privately, the girls thought it was pretty cold to be standing outside, but these people seemed to be prepared, all bundled up, some with small portable heaters to warm them.

"Are you looking for something special?" the woman asked.

"Yes," the girls replied, practically in unison. It was as if heaven had dropped these things here, just for them to buy.

"But we haven't got much time," Lia reminded them. "We want to get back before Kathy wakes up.

So the girls scurried from one table to the next. Jill and Maddy went together on a soft camel-color scarf that would look great with Kathy's coat, and Lia picked out a pair of dangly silver earrings to go with the necklace. Even though they were in a hurry, Erin took a bit longer. She didn't have as much money as her friends did, and she'd already spent some over the weekend. Still, she was determined to find something.

Then it caught her eye. It was a small gilt-framed sign, decorated with hand-painted roses and lettered in beautiful calligraphy. It read, THE BEST THINGS IN LIFE ARE FREE. LIKE FRIENDS.

"Oh," Erin said, "this will be perfect. I just hope Kathy knows I mean it."

When they got back to Zoe's, they peeked into the

living room and were disappointed to see Kathy's couch empty.

"She's awake," Jill groaned.

"I hear the shower. She must be in there."

Faster than they knew they could move, the girls raced around the kitchen, setting the table, putting the flowers in a vase, getting the food ready. By the time Kathy came out of the bathroom, dressed and ready for another angry encounter, everything was ready.

"I wish I had a camera," Jill giggled as she watched Kathy's expression change from angry, to shocked, to pleased.

"What is all this?" Kathy sputtered.

"Don't you think it's time you got a proper birthday party?" Lia asked.

"I sure do," Kathy said. "But I thought you guys had gone out and left me in the lurch again."

"Where did you think we went?" Maddy asked.

"I don't know. Just somewhere without me. I thought you were as mad as I was."

"No one else could be that mad," Jill said impishly.

"Hey, we deserved what you threw at us," Erin told her. "Me, especially, Kathy." Quietly she asked, "Can you forgive us?"

There was something about the way Erin asked, so humbly, that melted away the last bit of Kathy's anger. "Let's forget about it. Everyone does stuff they're sorry for."

"Well, we're sorry we didn't treat you and your birthday with the proper respect," Jill told her. "But we're going to rectify that right now."

And it did turn into quite a party. All the tension that had built up over the weekend dissipated in the laughter that the girls shared over breakfast. Zoe came out in her bathrobe to see what was going on, and even in her weakened state, got into the fun. When it came time to open the presents, Kathy looked shocked.

"Where did you get this?" she asked wonderingly as she ran her hand over the plush scarf. "You didn't have anything yesterday."

"A bunch of elves left it," Jill told her.

"Santa's elves," Maddy said. "Even *they* wanted to get some New York shopping in before Christmas."

"These are gorgeous," Kathy said as she opened the box with the silver necklace and earrings. She tried them on immediately.

Then she opened the last package. "Oh, Erin, it's beautiful," Kathy said. "The way it looks. And what it says."

"I really mean it, too," Erin said.

Kathy looked up at Erin. "I know you do."

Just then, the phone rang. Zoe picked it up, and a frown furrowed her brow. She put her hand over the receiver. "Kathy, are you expecting anyone?"

"Me? No."

"Well, the doorman says there's someone down-stairs to see you."

Kathy shrugged.

The doorman must have continued speaking be-cause Zoe said, "I see. Oh, I see. Uh-huh." Then, she hung up.

"So who was it?" Kathy wanted to know.

A small smile played around Zoe's lips. "You'll find out in a minute or two."

Kathy turned to her friends. "What do you know about this?" she demanded.

All the girls looked blank except Lia, who had a thought, then dismissed it as impossible.

"Should I answer the door when this mystery guest arrives?" Kathy asked.

"I don't see why not. You're the one who has the vis-itor."

Now Kathy began to look a bit nervous. The knock at the door brought her to her feet, but she didn't exactly hurry over to open it, until Zoe said, "Get going. You don't want your surprise to leave."

"Do you know who it is?" Jill asked Lia.

"It might be—"

"Rick!" Kathy squealed from the hallway. "What are you doing here?"

"It's your birthday isn't it?" he replied.

Kathy ushered him into the kitchen. Everyone started talking at once. Rick got hugs from his camp friends, he met Zoe, and Kathy still wanted to know how his visit came about.

"Okay," he said, sitting down at the kitchen table, now a mess of crumbs, wrappings, and dirty dishes and glasses. Quickly, he filled them in about Lia's call.

"Lia!" Kathy exclaimed.

"Hey, I just thought he was going to phone. I didn't expect an actual appearance."

"I was going to call, but since you were so close, well, my brother's been trying to get down here for a while. He had this photography exhibit he's been crazy to see. So we decided to just get up early and come down. It's less than a four-hour drive."

"I didn't know what happened to you," Kathy murmured. "It's like you just disappeared."

"It's been really hard to adjust to Boston," Rick said quietly. "I'm sorry, Kath, but I just haven't felt like talking much. Or writing for that matter."

"How long can you stay?" Kathy wanted to know.

"I've got the whole day."

"I hate to be a spoilsport, but we've got to leave for the airport by two," Zoe said.

"That still gives them a couple of hours," Maddy pointed out.

"Them?" Zoe asked.

"Rick did come here all the way from Boston," Jill added. "I think they're going to want some time alone."

"I can show you around," Kathy said happily.

Erin broke in. "Just don't ask to see Chinatown."

Everyone but Rick and Zoe thought that was uproariously funny. "I'll explain later," Kathy promised.

"Hey, we haven't had any birthday cake yet," Lia said. "Let's bring it out."

Kathy covered her face when Lia brought out a cake and candles and the group sang an off-tune chorus of "Happy Birthday." After they dug into the cake, Erin said, "You two should get going. Kathy, we'll pack up for you so you don't have to hurry back."

"You know, this birthday started out as one of the worst." She smiled at all of them. "Now it's one of the best."

"I bet the whole weekend's been something," Rick said, looking around the table. "The Holiday Five in New York. It's hard to believe the town is still standing."

"We haven't left yet," Erin shot back.

"We're going to make the most of our last couple of hours here, just like you two," Maddy added.

And that's just what they did.